1-10

D0065233

The Chopin Manuscript

**Center Point
Large Print**

Also by Jeffery Deaver
and available from Center Point Large Print:

Roadside Crosses
The Bodies Left Behind
The Broken Window
The Sleeping Doll
The Cold Moon
Praying for Sleep

**This Large Print Book carries the
Seal of Approval of N.A.V.H.**

BASED ON AN IDEA BY
JEFFERY DEAVER

The Chopin Manuscript

A SERIAL THRILLER

LEE CHILD
DAVID CORBETT
JEFFERY DEAVER
JOSEPH FINDER
JIM FUSILLI
JOHN GILSTRAP
JAMES GRADY
DAVID HEWSON
JOHN RAMSEY MILLER
P. J. PARRISH
RALPH PEZZULLO
S. J. ROZAN
LISA SCOTTOLINE
PETER SPIEGELMAN
ERICA SPINDLER

CENTER POINT PUBLISHING
THORNDIKE, MAINE

This Center Point Large Print edition
is published in the year 2010 by arrangement with
Writers House LLC.

The text of this Large Print edition is unabridged.
In other aspects, this book may vary
from the original edition.
Printed in the United States of America
on permanent paper.
Set in 16-point Times New Roman type.

ISBN: 978-1-60285-676-9

Library of Congress Cataloging-in-Publication Data

Deaver, Jeffery.
  The Chopin manuscript / based on an idea by Jeffery Deaver.
    p. cm.
  Co-written by Deaver and fourteen other authors each writing a chapter; conceived,
initiated, and completed by Deaver.
  ISBN 978-1-60285-676-9 (lib. bdg. : alk. paper)
  1. Chopin, Frédéric, 1810-1849--Manuscripts--Fiction.
   2. Music--Manuscripts--Fiction. 3. Large type books. I. Title.

PS3554.E1755C48 2010
813'.54--dc22

2009038933

Contents

Introduction

Your mission, if you choose to accept it, is to come up with an innovative idea to help put a brand new writers' organization on the map and then convince top thriller writers to donate their ideas and their time to make it work.

That was my main job when International Thriller Writers (ITW) was formed in October 2004 and I joined the founding board of directors.

As a thriller writer myself and owner of a marketing company for authors and publishers, the part of ITW's mission statement that was closest to my heart was: "To bestow recognition and promote the thriller genre at an innovative and superior level."

We came up with lists of ideas. Some fizzled right away. Others took a while to crash and burn. A few had some game and looked like they might actually come to fruition.

Of all possible projects, the idea of a serialized novel written by some of the genre's best writers— to be released first in audio—chapter by chapter over 15 weeks—was one of the most unusual and the one I was the most involved in coming up with and excited about.

Steve Feldberg, director of content at

Audible.com, and I hashed out the idea over the phone first and then over coffee in person. A few months later Audible gave the idea the green light and the ITW board announced it was on board.

That's when the impossible mission really started. How could I convince dozens of writers to donate their ideas and their time to a collaborative project that was different than anything done before?

Take a look at the cover of this book. We weren't just talking about writers . . . but wonderful writers, successful writers, writers who are used to actually getting paid (a lot of money) for their ideas, whose books are on national and international best-seller lists. Writers who are household names, who have sold millions of books. Writers who are all on deadline with their own books and who have commitments to their fans, publishers, and families.

How do you get Lee Child to abandon Jack Reacher? Get Jeff Deaver to write about someone other than Lincoln Rhyme? To get Lisa Scottoline to leave her beloved Philly? To get Jim Fusilli not only to write a chapter but take on the Herculean task of herding these big cats and running the show? And on and on with every one of the eleven other authors.

Turns out you pick up the phone and just ask.

Amazingly every author I asked to be part of this ground-breaking project said yes. Amazingly.

8

Eagerly. In fact so many said yes, I actually lost my own place in the book because I couldn't possibly take a spot that one of these luminaries was willing to fill.

The Chopin Manuscript—part one of *The Watchlist*—was the first ever audio serial thriller. It won the Best Audio Book of the Year and was an unqualified best-seller.

It was a unique collaboration among fifteen distinguished international thriller writers who came together with a single goal. To help establish ITW as a viable, valuable, important organization for its authors.

Jeffery Deaver conceived the characters and the setting and put the plot in motion with the first chapter. From there the story was turned over to fourteen authors who each wrote a chapter that propelled the story along. Along the way the plot took twists and turns as each author lent his or her own imprint on the tale. Characters were added as the action moved around the world—and the stakes got higher and higher. The book wrapped with Deaver writing the final two chapters, bringing The Chopin Manuscript to its explosive conclusion.

And then two years later everyone did it again (with a few new authors coming on board and a few who had prior commitments stepping out) with The Copper Bracelet (coming in April 2010 from Center Point Large Print).

Once again Deaver started it, a host of brilliant writers kept the story spinning and twisting and turning, and then Deaver finished it.

What you're holding in your hands is above all proof of how generous and talented the writers are who make up ITW. All of whom I want to thank for being part of a marvelous project that I hope you, dear reader, find as entertaining, breathtaking, thrilling, and un-put-down-able as I do.

M. J. Rose
July 2009

1

JEFFERY DEAVER

The piano tuner ran through ascending chords, enjoying the resistance of the heavy ivory keys. His balding head was bent forward, his eyes closed as he listened. The notes rose to the darkened ceiling of the recital hall near Warsaw's Old Market Square, then dissipated like smoke.

Satisfied with his work, the tuner replaced the temperament strips and his well-worn extension-tuning lever in their velvet case and indulged himself by playing a few minutes of Mozart, A Little Night Music, an ebullient piece that was one of his favorites.

Just as he concluded, the crisp sound of clapping palms echoed behind him and he spun around. Twenty feet away stood a man nodding and smiling. Stocky, with a flop of brown hair, broad of face. Southern Slavic, the tuner thought. He'd traveled in Yugoslavia many years ago.

"Lovely. Ah, my. So beautiful. Do you speak English?" the man asked with a thick accent.

"I do."

"Are you a performer here? You must be. You are so talented."

"Me? No, I simply tune pianos. But a tuner must

know his way about the keyboard too . . . Can I help you, sir? The recital hall is closed."

"Still, such a passion for music. I could hear it. Have you to perform?"

The piano tuner didn't particularly care to talk about himself, but he could discuss music all night long. He was, in addition to being perhaps the best piano tuner in Warsaw if not all of central Poland, an avid collector of recordings and original music manuscripts. If he'd had the means, he would collect instruments too. He had once played a Chopin polonaise at the very keyboard the composer had used; he considered it one of the highpoints of his life.

"I used to. But only in my youth." He told the man of his sweep through Eastern Europe with the Warsaw Youth Orchestra, with which he'd been second-chair cello.

He stared at the man, who in turn was examining the piano. "As I say, the hall is closed. But perhaps you're looking for someone?"

"I am, yes." The Slav walked closer and looked down. "Ah, a Bosendorfer. One of Germany's great contributions to culture."

"Oh, yes," the slight man said, caressing the black lacquer and gothic type of the company's name. "It's perfection. It truly is. Would you like to try it? Do you play?"

"Not like you. I wouldn't presume to even touch a single key after hearing your performance."

"You're too kind. You say you're looking for someone. You mean Anna? The French horn student? She was here earlier but I believe she's left. There's no one else, except the cleaning woman. But I can get a message to anyone in the orchestra or the administration, if you like."

The visitor stepped closer yet and gently brushed a key—true ivory, the piano having been made before the ban. "You, sir," he said, "are the one I came to see."

"Me? Do I know you?"

"I saw you earlier today."

"You did? Where? I don't recall."

"You were having lunch at a café overlooking that huge building. The fancy one, the biggest one in Warsaw. What is it?"

The piano tuner gave a laugh. "The biggest one in the country. The Palace of Culture and Science. A gift from the Soviets, which, the joke goes, they gave us in place of our freedom. Yes, I did have lunch there. But . . . Do I know you?"

The stranger stopped smiling. He looked from the piano into the narrow man's eyes.

Like the assault of the sudden vehement chord in Haydn's Surprise Symphony, fear struck the piano tuner. He picked up his tool kit and rose quickly. Then stopped. "Oh," he gasped. Behind the stranger he could see two bodies lying on the tile near the front door: Anna, the horn player; and beyond her, the cleaning woman. Two shadows on

13

the floor surrounded their limp figures, one from the entranceway light, one from their blood.

The Slav, not much taller than the piano tuner but far stronger, took him by the shoulders. "Sit," he whispered gently, pushing the man down on the bench then turning him to face the piano.

"What do you want?" A quaking voice, tears in his eyes.

"Shhh."

Shaking with fear, the piano tuner thought madly, What a fool I am! I should have fled the moment the man commented on the Bosendorfer's German ancestry. Anyone with a true understanding of the keyboard knew the instruments are made in Austria.

When he was stopped at Krakow's John Paul II airport, he was certain his offense had to do with what he carried in his briefcase.

The hour was early and he'd wakened much earlier at the Pod Roza, "Under the Rose," which was his favorite hotel in Poland, owing both to its quirky mix of scrolly ancient and starkly modern, and to the fact that Franz Liszt had stayed there. Still half asleep, without his morning coffee or tea, he was startled from his stupor by the two uniformed men who appeared over him.

"Mr. Harold Middleton?"

He looked up. "Yes, that's me." And suddenly realized what had happened. When airport security had looked through his attaché case, they'd seen it and grown concerned. But out of prudence the young guards there had chosen not to say anything. They let him pass, then called for reinforcements: these two large, unsmiling men.

Of the twenty or so passengers in the lounge awaiting the bus to take them to the Lufthansa flight to Paris, some people looked his way—the younger ones. The older, tempered by the Soviet regime, dared not. The man closest to Middleton, two chairs away, glanced up involuntarily with a flash of ambiguous concern on his face, as if he might be mistaken as his companion. Then, realizing he wasn't going to be questioned, he turned back to his newspaper, obviously relieved.

"You will please to come with us. This way. Yes. Please." Infinitely polite, the massive guard nodded back toward the security line.

"Look, I know what this is about. It's simply a misunderstanding." He larded his voice with patience, respect and good nature. It was the tone you had to take with local police, the tone you used talking your way through border crossings. Middleton nodded at the briefcase. "I can show you some documentation that—"

The second, silent guard picked up the case.

The other: "Please. You will come." Polite but inflexible. This young, square-jawed man who seemed incapable of smiling held his eye firmly and there was no debate. The Poles, Middleton knew, had been the most willful resisters of the Nazis.

Together they walked back through the tiny, largely deserted airport, the taller guards flanking the shorter, nondescript American. At 56, Harold Middleton carried a few more pounds than he had last year, which itself had seen a weight gain of a few pounds over the prior. But curiously his weight—conspiring with his thick black hair—made him appear younger than he was. Only five years ago, at his daughter's college graduation, the girl had introduced him to several of her classmates as her brother. Everyone in the group had bought the deception. Father and daughter had laughed about that many times since.

He thought of her now and hoped fervently he wouldn't miss his flight and the connection to Washington, D.C. He was going to have dinner with Charlotte and her husband that night at Tyson's Corner. It was the first time he'd see her since she announced her pregnancy.

But as he looked past security at the awaiting cluster of men—also unsmiling—he had a despairing feeling that dinner might be postponed. He wondered for how long.

They walked through the exit line and joined the group: two more uniformed officers and a middle-aged man in a rumpled brown suit under a rumpled brown raincoat.

"Mr. Middleton, I am Deputy Inspector Stanieski, with the Polish National Police, Krakow region." No ID was forthcoming.

The guards hemmed him in, as if the 5-foot, 10-inch American was going to karate kick his way to freedom.

"I will see your passport please."

He handed over the battered, swollen blue booklet. Stanieski looked it over and glanced at the picture, then at the man in front of him twice. People often had trouble seeing Harold Middleton, couldn't remember what he looked like. A friend of his daughter said he would make a good spy; the best ones, the young man explained, are invisible. Middleton knew this was true; he wondered how Charlotte's friend did.

"I don't have much time until that flight."

"You will not make the flight, Mr. Middleton. No. We will be returning to Warsaw."

Warsaw? Two hours away.

"That's crazy. Why?"

No answer.

He tried once more. "This is about the manuscript, isn't it?" He nodded to the attaché case. "I can explain. The name Chopin is on it, yes, but I'm convinced it's a forgery. It's not valuable. It's not a national treasure. I've been asked to take it to the United States to finish my analysis. You can call Doctor—"

The inspector shook his head. "Manuscript? No,

17

Mr. Middleton. This is not about a manuscript. It's about a murder."

"Murder?"

The man hesitated. "I use the word to impress on you the gravity of the situation. Now it is best that I say nothing more, and I would strongly suggest you do the same, isn't it?"

"My luggage—"

"Your luggage is already in the car. Now." A nod of his head toward the front door. "We will go."

"Please, come in, Mr. Middleton. Sit. Yes there is good . . . I am Jozef Padlo, first deputy inspector with the Polish National Police." This time an ID was exhibited, but Middleton got the impression the gaunt man, about his own age and much taller, was flashing the card only because Middleton expected it and that the formality was alien in Polish law enforcement.

"What's this all about, Inspector? Your man says murder and tells me nothing more."

"Oh, he mentioned that?" Padlo grimaced. "Krakow. They don't listen to us there. Slightly better than Posnan, but not much."

They were in an off-white office, beside a window that looked out on the gray spring sky. There were many books, computer printouts, a few maps and no decorations other than official citations, an incongruous ceramic cactus wearing a cowboy hat and pictures of the man's wife and

18

children and grandchildren. Many pictures. They seemed like a happy family. Middleton thought again of his daughter.

"Am I being charged with anything?"

"Not at this point." His English was excellent and Middleton wasn't surprised to notice that there was a certificate on the wall testifying to Padlo's completion of a course in Quantico and one at the Law Enforcement Management Institute of Texas.

Oh, and the cactus.

"Then I can leave."

"You know, we have anti-smoking laws here. I think that's your doing, your country's. You give us Burger King and take away our cigarettes." The inspector shrugged and lit a Sobieski. "No, you can't leave. Now, please, you had lunch yesterday with a Henryk Jedynak, a piano tuner."

"Yes. Henry . . . Oh no. Was he the one murdered?"

Padlo watched Middleton carefully. "I'm afraid he was, yes. Last night. In the recital hall near Old Market Square."

"No, no . . ." Middleton didn't know the man well—they'd met only on this trip—but they'd hit it off immediately and had enjoyed each other's company. He was shocked by the news of Jedynak's death.

"And two other people were killed, as well. A musician and a cleaning woman. Stabbed to death. For no reason, apparently, other than they had the misfortune to be there at the same time as the killer."

"This is terrible. But why?"

"Have you known Mr. Jedynak long?"

"No. We met in person for the first time yesterday. We'd emailed several times. He was a collector of manuscripts."

"Manuscripts? Books?"

"No. Musical manuscripts—the handwritten scores. And he was involved with the Chopin Museum."

"At Ostrogski Castle." The inspector said this as if he'd heard of the place but never been there.

"Yes. I had a meeting yesterday afternoon with the director of the Czartoryski Museum in Krakow, and I asked Henry to brief me about him and their collection. It was about a questionable Chopin score."

Padlo showed no interest in this. "Tell me, please, about your meeting. In Warsaw."

"Well, I met Henry for coffee in the late morning at the museum, he showed me the new acquisitions in the collection. Then we returned downtown and had lunch at a café. I can't remember where."

"The Frederick Restaurant."

That's how Padlo found him, he supposed—an entry in Jedynak's PDA or diary. "Yes, that was it. And then we went our separate ways. I took the train to Krakow."

"Did you see anyone following you or watching you at lunch?"

"Why would someone follow us?"

Padlo inhaled long on his cigarette. When he wasn't puffing he lowered his hand below his desk. "Did you see anyone?" he repeated.

"No."

He nodded. "Mr. Middleton, I must tell you . . . I regret I have to but it is important. Your friend was tortured before he died. I won't go into the details, but the killer used some piano string in very unpleasant ways. He was gagged so the screams could not be heard but his right hand was uninjured, presumably so that he could write whatever this killer demanded of him. He wanted information."

"My God . . ." Middleton closed his eyes briefly, recalling Henry's showing pictures of his wife and two sons.

"I wonder what that might be," Padlo said. "This piano tuner was well known and well liked. He was also a very transparent man. Musician, tradesman, husband and father. There seemed to be nothing dark about his life . . ." A careful examination of Middleton's face. "But perhaps the killer thought that was not the case. Perhaps the killer thought he had a second life involving more than music . . ." With a nod, he added, "Somewhat like you."

"What're you getting at?"

"Tell me about your other career, please."

"I don't have another career. I teach music and authenticate music manuscripts."

"But you had another career recently."

"Yes, I did. But what's that got to do with anything?"

Padlo considered this for a moment, and said, "Because certain facts have come into alignment."

A cold laugh. "And what exactly does that mean?" This was the most emotional Harold Middleton usually got. He believed that you gave up your advantage when you lost control. That's what he told himself, though he doubted that he was even capable of losing control.

"Tell me about that career, Colonel. Do some people still call you that, 'Colonel'?"

"Not anymore. But why are you asking me questions you already seem to know the answers to?"

"I know a few things. I'm curious to know more. For instance, I only know that you were connected with the ICTY and the ICCt, but not many details."

The UN-sanctioned International Criminal Tribunal for the Former Yugoslavia investigated and tried individuals for war crimes committed during the complicated and tragic fighting among the Serbs, Bosnians, Croatians and Albanian ethnic groups in the 1990s. The ICCt was the International Criminal Court, established in 2002 to try war criminals for crimes in any area of the world. Both were located in The Hague in Holland, and had been created because nations tended to quickly forget about the atrocities committed within their borders and were reluctant to find and try those who'd committed them.

"How did you end up working for them? It seems a curious leap from your country's army to an international tribunal."

"I was planning to retire anyway. I'd been in the service for more than two decades."

"But still. Please."

Middleton decided that cooperation was the only way that would let him leave anytime soon. With the time difference he still had a chance to get into D.C. in time for a late supper at the Ritz Carlton with his daughter and son-in-law.

He explained to the inspector briefly that he had been a military intelligence officer with the 7,000 U.S. troops sent to Kosovo in the summer of 1999 as part of the peacekeeping force when the country was engaged in the last of the Yugoslavian wars. Middleton was based at Camp Broadsteel in the southeast of the country, the sector America oversaw. The largely rural area, dominated by Mount Duke which rose like Fuji over the rugged hills, was an ethnically Albanian area, as was most of Kosovo, and had been the site of many incursions by Serbs—both from other parts of Kosovo and from Milosevic's Serbia, which Kosovo had been part of. The fighting was largely over—the tens of thousands of ironically dubbed "humanitarian" bombing strikes had had their desired effect—but the peacekeepers on the ground were still on high alert to stop clashes between the infamous Serb guerillas and the equally ruthless Albanian Kosovo Liberation Army forces.

Padlo took this information in, nodding as he lit another cigarette.

"Not long after I was deployed there, the base commander got a call from a general in the British sector, near Pristina, the capital. He'd found something interesting and had been calling all the international peacekeepers to see if anyone had a background in art collecting."

"And why was that?" Padlo stared at the Sobieski hidden below eye-level.

The smell was not as terrible as Middleton had expected, but the office was filling with smoke. His eyes stung. "Let me give you some background. It goes back to World War Two."

"Please, tell me."

"Well, many Albanians from Kosovo fought with an SS unit—the Twenty-First Waffen Mountain Division. Their main goal was eliminating partisan guerillas, but it also gave them the chance to ethnically cleanse the Serbs, who had been their enemies for years."

A grimace appeared on the inspector's heavily lined face. "Ah, it's always the same story wherever you look. Poles versus the Russians. Arabs versus the Jews. Americans versus"—a smile—"everyone."

Middleton ignored him. "The Twenty-First supposedly had another job too. With the fall of Italy and an Allied invasion a sure thing, Himmler and Goering and other Nazis who'd been looting art from Eastern Europe wanted secure places to hide it—so that even if Germany fell, the Allies couldn't find it. The Twenty-First reportedly brought truckloads to Kosovo. Made sense. A small, little populated, out-of-the-mainstream country. Who'd think to look there for a missing Cezanne or Manet?

"What the British general had found was an old Eastern Orthodox church. It was abandoned years ago and being used as a dormitory for displaced Serbs by a U.N. relief organization. In the basement his soldiers unearthed 50 or 60 boxes of rare books, paintings and music folios."

"My, that many?"

"Oh, yes. A lot was damaged, some beyond repair, but other items were virtually untouched. I didn't know much about the paintings or the books, but I'd studied music history in college and I've collected recordings and manuscripts for years. I got the okay to fly up and take a look."

"And what did you find?"

"Oh, it was astonishing. Original pieces by Bach and his sons, Mozart, Handel, sketches by Wagner—some of them had never been seen before. I was speechless."

"Valuable?"

"Well, you can't really put a dollar value on a find like that. It's the cultural benefit, not the financial."

"But still, worth millions?"

"I suppose."

"What happened then?"

"I reported what I'd found to the British and to my general, and he cleared it with Washington for me to stay there for a few days and catalog what I could. Good press, you know."

"True in police work too." The cigarette got crushed out forcefully under a yellow thumb, as if Padlo were quitting forever.

Middleton explained that that night he took all the manuscripts and folios that he could carry back to British quarters in Pristina and worked for hours cataloging and examining what he'd found.

"The next morning I was very excited, wondering what else I'd find. I got up early to return . . ."

The American stared at a limp yellow file folder on the inspector's desktop, the one with three faded checkmarks on it. He looked up and heard Padlo say, "The church was St. Sophia."

"You know about it?" Middleton was surprised. The incident had made the news but by then—with the world focusing on the millennium and the Y2K crisis, the Balkans had become simply a footnote to fading history.

"Yes, I do. I didn't realize you were involved."

Middleton remembered walking to the church and thinking, I must've gotten up pretty damn early if none of the refugees were awake yet, especially with all the youngsters living there. Then he paused, wondering where the British guards were. Two had been stationed outside the church the day before. Just at that moment he saw a window open on the second floor and a teenage girl look out, her long hair obscuring half her face. She was calling, "Green shirt, green shirt . . . Please . . . Green shirt."

He hadn't understood. But then it came to him. She was referring to his fatigues and was calling for his help.

"What was it like?" Padlo asked softly.

Middleton merely shook his head.

The inspector didn't press him for details. He asked, "And Rugova was the man responsible?"

He was even more surprised that the inspector knew about the former Kosovo Liberation Army commander Agim Rugova. That fact was not learned until later, long after Rugova and his men had fled from Pristina, and the story of St. Sophia had grown stone cold.

"Your change in career is making sense now, Mr. Middleton. After the war you became an investigator to track him down."

"That's it in a nutshell." He smiled as if that could flick away the cached memories, clear as computer jpegs, of that morning.

Middleton had returned to Camp Broadsteel and served out his rotation, spending most of his free time running intelligence reports on Rugova and the many other war criminals the torn region had spawned. Back at the Pentagon, he'd done the same. But it wasn't the U.S. military's job to catch them and bring them to trial, and he made no headway.

So when he retired, he set up an operation in a small Northern Virginia office park. He called it "War Criminal Watch" and spent his days on the phone and computer, tracking Rugova and others. He made contacts at the ICTY and worked with them regularly but they and the UN's tactical operation were busy with bigger fish—like Ratko Mladic, Naser Oric and others involved in the Srebrenica massacre, the worst atrocity in Europe since World War II, and Milosevic himself. Middleton would come up with a lead and it would founder. Still he couldn't get St. Sophia out of his mind.

Green shirt, green shirt . . . Please . . .

He decided that he couldn't be effective working from America nor working alone. So after some months of searching he found people who'd help: two American soldiers who'd been in Kosovo and helped him in the investigation at St. Sophia and a woman humanitarian worker from Belgrade he'd met in Pristina.

The overworked ICTY was glad to accept them

as independent contractors, working with the Prosecutor's Office. They became known in the ICTY as "The Volunteers."

Lespasse and Brocco, the soldiers, younger, driven by their passion for the hunt;

Leonora Tesla, by her passion to rid the world of sorrow, a passion that made the otherwise-common woman beautiful;

And the elder, Harold Middleton, a stranger to passion and driven by . . . well, even he couldn't say what. The intelligence officer who never seemed to be able to process the HUMINT on himself.

Unarmed—at least as far as the ICTY and local law enforcement knew—they managed to track down several of Rugova's henchmen and, through them, finally the man himself, who was living in a shockingly opulent townhouse in Nice, France, under a false identity. The arrangement was that, for ethical reasons, the Volunteers' job was solely to provide the tribunal with intelligence and contacts; the SFOR, the UN's Stabilization Force—the military operation in charge of apprehending former Yugoslav war criminals—and local police, to the extent they were cooperative, would be the arresting agents.

In 2002, working on pristine data provided by Middleton and his crew, UN and French troops raided the townhouse and arrested Rugova.

Tribunal trials are interminable, but three years

later he was convicted for crimes that occurred at St. Sophia. He was appealing his conviction while living in what was, in Middleton's opinion, a far-too-pleasant detention center in The Hague.

Middleton could still picture the swarthy man at trial, ruggedly handsome, confident and indignant, swearing that he'd never committed genocide or ethnic cleansing. He admitted he was a soldier but said that what happened at St. Sophia was merely an "isolated incident" in an unfortunate war. Middleton told this to the inspector.

"Isolated incident," Padlo whispered.

"It makes the horror far worse, don't you think? Phrasing it so antiseptically."

"I do, yes." Another draw on the cigarette.

Middleton wished that he had a candy bar, his secret passion.

Padlo then asked, "I'm curious about one thing—was Rugova acting on anyone else's orders, do you think? Was there someone he reported to?"

Middleton's attention coalesced instantly at this question. "Why do you ask that?" he asked sharply.

"Was he?"

The American debated and decided to continue to cooperate. For the moment. "When we were hunting for him we heard rumors that he was backed by someone. It made sense. His KLA outfit had the best weapons of any unit in the country, even better than some of the regular Serbian troops. They were the best trained, and they could hire pilots for helicopter extractions. That was unheard of in Kosovo. There were rumors of large amounts of cash. And he didn't seem to take orders from any of the known KLA senior commanders. But we had only one clue that there was somebody behind him. A message had been left for him about a bank deposit. It was hidden in a copy of Goethe's Faust we found in an apartment in Eze."

"Any leads?"

"We thought possibly British or American. Maybe Canadian. Some of the phrasing in the note suggested it."

"No idea of his name?"

"No. We gave him a nickname, after the book—Faust."

"A deal with the devil. Are you still searching for this man?"

"Me? No. My group disbanded. The Tribunal's still in force and the prosecutors and EUFOR might be looking for him but I doubt it. Rugova's in jail, some of his associates too. There are bigger fish to fry. You know that expression?"

"No, but I understand." Padlo crushed out another cigarette. "You're young. Why did you quit this job? The work seems important."

"Young?" Middleton smiled. Then it faded. He said only, "Events intervened."

"Another dispassionate phrase, that one. 'Events intervened.' "

Middleton looked down.

"An unnecessary comment on my part. Forgive me. I owe you answers and you'll now understand why I asked what I did." He hit a button on his phone and spoke in Polish. Middleton knew enough to understand he was asking for some photographs.

Padlo disconnected and said, "In investigating the murder of the piano tuner I learned that you were probably the last person—well, second last—to see him alive. Your name and hotel phone number were in his address book for that day. I ran your name through Interpol and our other databases and found about your involvement with the tribunals. There was a brief reference to Agim Rugova, but a cross-reference in Interpol as well, which had been added only late yesterday."

"Yesterday?"

"Yes. Rugova died yesterday. The apparent cause of death was poisoning."

Middleton felt his heart pound. Why hadn't anyone called? Then he realized that he was no longer connected with the ICTY and that it had been years since St. Sophia was on anyone's radar screen.

An isolated incident . . .

"This morning I called the prison and learned that Rugova had approached a guard several weeks ago about bribing his way out of prison. He offered a huge amount of money. 'Where would he, an

32

impoverished war criminal, get such funds?' the guard asked. He said his wife could get the amount he named—one hundred thousand euros. The guard reported the matter and there it rested. But then, four days ago, Rugova had a visitor—a man with a fake name and fake ID, as it turned out. After he leaves Rugova falls ill and yesterday dies of poison. The police go to the wife's house to inform her and find she's been dead for several days. She was stabbed."

Dead . . . Middleton felt a fierce urge to call Leonora and tell her.

"When I learned of your connection with the piano tuner and the death on the same day of the war criminal you'd had arrested, I had sent to me a prison security camera picture of the probable murderer. I showed the picture to a witness we located who saw the likely suspect leaving the Old Market Square recital hall last night."

"It's the same man?"

"She said with certainty that it was." Padlo indulged again and lit a Sobieski. "You seem to be the hub of this strange wheel, Mr. Middleton. A man kills Rugova and his wife and then tortures and kills a man you've just met with. So, now, you and I are entwined in this matter."

It was then that a young uniformed officer arrived carrying an envelope. He placed it on the inspector's desk.

"Dzenkuje," Padlo said.

The aide nodded and, after glancing at the American, vanished.

The inspector handed the photos to Middleton, who looked down at them. "Oh, my God." He sucked cigarette-smoke-tainted air deep into his lungs.

"What?" Padlo asked, seeing his reaction. "Was he someone you know from your investigation of Rugova?"

The American looked up. "This man . . . He was sitting next to me at Krakow airport. He was taking my flight to Paris." The man in the ugly checked jacket.

"No! Are you certain?"

"Yes. He must've killed Henryk to find out where I was going."

And in a shocking instant it was clear. Someone—this man or Faust, or perhaps he was Faust—was after Middleton and the other Volunteers.

Why? For revenge? Did he fear something? Was there some other reason? And why would he kill Rugova?

The American jabbed his finger at the phone. "Did he get on the flight to Paris? Has it landed? Find out now."

Padlo's tongue touched the corner of his mouth. He lifted the receiver and spoke in such rapid Polish that Middleton couldn't follow the conversation.

Finally the inspector hung up. "Yes, it's landed and everyone has disembarked. Other than you, everyone with a boarding pass was on the flight. But after that? They don't know. They'll check the flight manifest against passport control at De Gaulle—if he left the airport. And outgoing flight manifests in case he continued in transit."

Middleton shook his head. "He's changed identity by now. He saw me detained and he's using a new passport."

The inspector said, "He could be on his way to anywhere in the world."

But he wasn't, Middleton knew. The only question was this: Was he en route to Africa to find Tesla at her relief agency? Or to the States, where Lespasse ran a very successful computer company and Brocco edited the Human Rights Observer newsletter?

Or was he on a different flight headed to D.C., where Middleton himself lived?

Then his legs went weak.

As he recalled that, showing off proud pictures, he'd told the piano tuner that his daughter lived in the D.C. area.

What a lovely young woman, and her husband, so handsome. . . . They seem so happy.

Middleton leapt to his feet. "I have to get home. And if you try to stop me, I'll call the embassy." He strode toward the door.

"Wait," Padlo said sharply.

Middleton spun around. "I'm warning you. Do not try to stop me. If you do—"

"No, no, I only mean. . . . Here." He stepped forward and handed the American his passport. Then he touched Middleton's arm. "Please. I want this man too. He killed three of my citizens. I want him badly. Remember that."

He believed the inspector said something else but by then Middleton was jogging hard down the endless hall, as gray as the offices, as gray as the sky, digging into his pocket for his cell phone.

2

DAVID HEWSON

Felicia Kaminski first noticed the tramp outside the Pantheon when she was playing gypsy folk tunes, old Roman favorites, anything that could put a few coins in the battered gray violin case she had inherited from her mother, along with the century-old, sweet-toned Italian instrument that lived inside. The man listened for more than 10 minutes, watching her all the time. Then he walked up close, so close she could smell the cloud of sweat and humanity that hung around people of the street, not that they ever seemed to notice.

"I wanna hear 'Volarè,'" he grumbled in English, his voice rough and carrying an accent she couldn't quite place. He held a crumpled and dirt-stained 10-euro note. He was perhaps 35, though it was difficult to be precise. He stood at least six feet tall, muscular, almost athletic, though the thought seemed ridiculous.

"'Volarè' is a song, sir, not a piece of violin music," she responded, with more teenage ungraciousness than was, perhaps, wise.

His face, as much as she could see behind the black unkempt beard, seemed sharp and observant. More so, it occurred to her, than most street people who were either elderly Italians thrown out of their

37

homes by harsh times, or foreign clandestini, Iraqis, Africans and all manner of nationalities from the Balkans, each keeping their own counsel, each trying to pursue their own particular course through the dark, half-secret hidden economy for those trying to survive without papers.

There were other more pressing reasons that made hers a bold and unwise response. The money her uncle had given her had not been much to begin with, though more generous than his meager living as a Warsaw piano tuner ought to have allowed. Two months before, on the day she turned 19, he had abruptly announced that his role as her guardian was finished, and that it was time to seek a new life in the west. She chose Italy because she wanted warm weather and beauty, and refused to follow the stream of Poles migrating to England. The grubby, slow bus to Rome had cost 50 euros, and the room in a squalid student house in San Giovanni swallowed up a further 200 each week, as did the language-school lessons in Italian. Her adequate English meant she could get some bar work but only in tourist dives at what the owners called "the Polish rate"—four euros an hour, less than the legal minimum wage. She ate like a sparrow, pizza rustica, precooked, often disgusting, but less than two euros a slice. She never went out and had yet to make a friend. Still each week the money from Uncle Henryk went down a little further. She could not, in all conscience, call and ask for more.

"I know it's a song," the tramp replied with an unpleasant sneer on his half-hidden face. Then he crooned a line of it, in the voice of a long-dead American singer she'd heard when her mother and father played music on their cheap hi-fi to remind themselves of their days in the States, before they returned to a new, free Poland in search of different lives. The name of the singer came back to her: Dean Martin. And the tune too, so she played it, pitch perfect, from memory, improvising a little after the fashion of Stéphane Grappelli, putting a leisurely jazz swing on each inflected run of notes until the original was only just recognizable.

She was good at the fiddle. Sometimes, if she was bored or there seemed to be someone musical in her audience, she would pull out some sheet music stuffed into the case, ask a spectator to hold it, then play Wieniawski's Obertass mazurka, with its leaping fireworks of double stopping, harmonics and left-hand pizzicato. Both of her parents were musical, her mother a violinist, her father an accomplished pianist. Together they had provided her with a musical education from before she could remember, in a household where music was as natural and easy as laughter, right up until the black day they disappeared and she found herself under the wing of Uncle Henryk.

The tramp stared at her as if she'd committed a sin.

"You screwed with it," he spat. "Bad girl. You

ought to know your place." He stared at his own clothes: a grimy overcoat that stank of sweat and urine, with a belt made, perhaps a little theatrically, out of rope. "One little step up from me. Nothing more."

Then he threw a single euro in her violin case and stomped off toward Largo Argentina, the open space where she used to catch the bus back home, fascinated always by the wrecked collection of ancient temples there—a ragged, shapeless gathering of columns and stones populated by a yowling community of feral cats, a piece of history only she and the passing tourists seemed to notice any more. She didn't like cats. They were bold, aggressive, insistent, climbing into her fiddle case when it was open to collect money. So she kept a small water pistol, modeled on something military, alongside her music and rosin, and used it to shoo them away when the creatures became too persistent.

The bum caught up with her four times after that. Twice at the Trevi Fountain. Once in the Campo dei Fiori. Once outside the new museum for the Ara Pacis, the peace monument erected by Augustus that now lived in a modern, cubist home by the hectic road running alongside the Tiber. She was surprised to see him there. It didn't seem the usual kind of place for street people, and she caught him staring through the windows, engrossed in the beautifully carved monument inside she had only glimpsed from the street too, since paying the entrance fee was beyond her. Homeless men rarely looked at Imperial Roman statuary, she thought. Most of them never looked much at anything at all.

And now he was back near her again—on this hot, sunny summer morning in the Via delle Botteghe Oscure at the weekly market her uncle had told her about. It took place at the foot of the Via dei Polacchi—the street of Poles—and made her homesick every time she went. This was where the poor, migrant Polish community gathered in an impromptu bazaar that was part economic necessity, part reaffirmation of their distant roots. There were cars and vans, all rusty, all belching diesel as they arrived bearing plates from Warsaw and Gdansk. Quickly, not wishing to draw the attention of the police, they threw open their doors and trunks and began selling all the goods that Polish immigrants could not find or, more likely, afford in their new home: spirits and sausage, ham and pastries; some clearly homemade, a few possibly illegal.

Felicia knew none of these people. But sometimes the poor were the most generous, particularly when they knew she was Polish too, alone in the city, still a little lost. The Berlin Wall had tumbled to the ground when she was 12 months old, an infant in some small apartment in a suburb of Chicago. She knew this because her parents had told her so often of the joy that followed. Of their

41

own expectant return to the country they had fled in order to throw off the shackles of Communism.

There had always been a shadow in their eyes when they spoke of that decision. As she grew older she knew why. When they left Poland it was a world of black and white, and they returned to one that was a shifting shade of gray. The bad days before she was born was a time of secret police and cruel, arbitrary punishment of dissent, but no one had to travel thousands of miles to a distant country to earn a living. They said something good had been lost alongside the visible, more easily acknowledged bad. Talking to the old men and women who gathered at the foot of the Via dei Polacchi she had come to realize there was a gulf between them and her that could never be bridged, a strange sense of guilty loss she could never share. Yet there was a bond too. She was Polish, she was poor. When she played the right notes—a mazurka, a polonaise—there were misty eyes all around and a constant shower of small coins into the fiddle case.

And on this day there was the tramp too, with a hateful look in his eyes, one that said, she believed . . . shame on you, shame on you.

As she bowed a slow country dance she told herself that, if he continued with these attentions, she would upbraid him, loudly, in public, with no fear. Who was a tramp to talk to anyone of shame? What gave him the right? . . .

Then, feeling a hand on her shoulder, she ceased playing and turned to find herself staring into the amiable, bright blue eyes of a middle-aged man in a gray suit. He had a pale, fleshy face with stubbly red cheeks, receding fair hair and the easy, confident demeanor of someone official, like a civil servant or a school headmaster.

"You play beautifully, Felicia," he said in Polish.

"Do I know you?"

He took out an ID card from his jacket and flashed it in front of her face, too quickly for her to make much sense of the words there.

"No. I am a Polish police officer on attachment here in Rome. There is no need for you to know me."

She must have looked startled. He placed a hand on her arm and said, in a voice full of reassurance, "Do not be alarmed. There is nothing for you to worry about." His genial face fell. "I am simply performing an unhappy task which falls to this profession from time to time. Come, I will buy coffee. There is a small place around the corner."

The man had such a pleasant air of authority that she followed him automatically into the Via dei Polacchi, even though she couldn't remember any cafe in this direction.

They were halfway along when he stopped her in the shadow of an overhanging building. There was such sadness in his eyes, a sense of regret too.

"I am sorry," he said in his low, calm voice.

"There is no easy way to say this. Your uncle Henryk has been killed."

Her stomach clenched. Her eyes began to sting. "Killed?"

"Murdered, as he worked. With two other people too. Such a world we live in."

"In Warsaw?"

He shrugged. "This would never have happened before. Not in the old days. People then had too much respect. Too much fear."

There were so many questions, and none of them would form themselves into a sensible sentence in Felicia's mind. "I must go home," she said finally.

The man was silent for a moment, thinking, a different expression in his eyes, one she couldn't work out.

"You can't afford to go home," he observed, frowning. "What's there for you anyway? It was never your country. Not really."

The narrow street was empty. A cloud had skittered across the bright summer sun casting the entire area into sudden gloom.

"I can afford a bus ride," she answered, suddenly cross.

"No you can't," he replied, and took her by both arms. He was strong. His blue eyes now burned, insistent, demanding. "What did your uncle give you? To come here?"

She tried to shake herself free. It was impossible. His grip was too firm.

"Some money . . . Two thousand euros. It was all he had."

"Not money," the man barked at her, his voice rising in volume. "I'm not talking money."

He turned his elbow so that his forearm fell beneath her throat and pinned her against the wall as he snatched her fiddle case with his free hand. Then he quickly bent down, flipped up the single latch with his teeth and scrabbled open the lid.

"This is a pauper's instrument," he grumbled, and flinging the fiddle to the ground. Crumpled sheets of music followed, fluttering to the cobblestones like leaves in autumn. "What did he give you?"

"Nothing. Nothing . . ."

She stopped. He had discarded the bow and her last piece of rosin, and now had her one remaining spare string, a Thomastik-Infeld Dominant A, in his fingers. He took away his elbow. Before she could run off, he jerked her back and punched her hard in the stomach. The breath disappeared from her lungs. Tears of pain and rage and fear rose in her eyes.

As she began to recover, she saw he had turned the fiddle string into a noose and felt it slip over her head, pushing it down until it rested on her neck. He pulled it, not so tight, only so much that she could feel the familiar wound metal become a cold ligature around her throat.

"Poor little lost girl," he whispered, his breath

rank and hot in her ear. "No home. No friends. No future. One last time . . . What did he give you?"

"Nothing . . . Nothing . . ."

The Thomastik-Infeld Dominant A started to tighten. She was aware of her own breathing, the short, repetitive muscular motion one always took for granted. His face grew huge in her vision. He was smiling. This was, she now realized, the result he wished all along.

Then the smile faded. A low, animal grunt issued from his mouth. His body fell forward, crushing hers against the wall, and a crimson spurt of blood began to gush from between his clenched teeth. She turned her head to avoid the red stream now flowing down his chin, and clawed at the noose on her throat, loosening it, forcing the deadly loop over her hair until it was free and she could manage to drag it over her head.

Something thrust the gray-suited man aside. The tramp was there. A long stiletto knife sat in his right fist, its entire length red with gore.

He dropped the weapon and held out his hand.

"Come with me now," he said. "There are three of them in a car round the corner. They won't wait long."

"Who are you?" she mumbled, her head reeling, breath still short.

A car was starting to turn into the narrow street, finding it too difficult to make the corner in one go. The cloud worked free of the sun. Bright, blinding light filled the area around them, enough to make their presence known. She heard Polish voices and other accents, ones she didn't recognize. They sounded angry.

"If you stay here you will die," the tramp insisted. "Like your uncle. Like your mother and your father. Come with me . . ."

She bent down and picked up her fiddle and bow, roughly pushing them into the case, along with the scrappy sheets of music.

And then they ran.

He had a scooter round the corner. A brand new purple Vespa with a rental sticker on the rear mudguard. She climbed on the back automatically, hanging tight, the fiddle case still in her grip, as he roared through the narrow lanes trying to lose the vehicle behind.

It wasn't easy. She turned her head and saw the car bouncing off the ancient stone walls of the quarter, following them down narrow alleys the wrong way. She knew this area. It was one of her favorites for its unexpected sights and the way the buildings ranged across the centuries, sometimes as far back as the age of Caesar.

He was going the wrong way and she knew it but they were there before she could tell him. The Vespa screamed to a halt in a dead-end alley sealed off by freshly painted black iron railings, a view point over the tangled ruins around the Pescaria, the imperial fish market that led to the vast circular stump of the Theatre of Marcellus, like some smaller Colosseum cut short by a giant's knife. There was no road, only a narrow pathway down into the mess of columns and shattered walls.

They ran and stumbled across threadbare grass through the low petrified forest of dusty granite and marble. She could hear shouts behind and anguished cries in Polish. Then she heard a shot. The tramp's strong hand grasped her as she tripped over a fluted portion of shattered column. Panting for breath, she found herself in the angry mass of traffic beneath the looming theatre. He dragged her into the mob of vehicles. Halfway across the road there was a young man on a scooter, long black hair falling out from beneath his helmet.

The tramp kicked him out of the seat, then screamed at her to get onto the pillion.

She didn't need to think any more. She didn't want to. They wound a sinuous route through the snarled-up vehicles, found the sidewalk on the river side of the road, roared over the cobbles, out to the Lungotevere. The traffic was just as bad there.

She dared to turn. Over the road, fighting through the cars, were three men, guns in their hands.

She swore. She prayed. And then they were through, on the Tiber side of the road, rattling down the steps that led down to the water and the long broad concrete of the flood defenses.

Two days before she'd walked here, wondering, thinking, trying to work out where she belonged. Not yet 20, born in a country that had forgotten her, without parents. And now, she reflected, without her uncle who had come to her rescue when she found herself orphaned. She clung on, tears in her eyes, determined they'd be spent before this man who had both rescued and kidnapped her would look into her face again.

After half a mile, they raced up a long walkway and returned to the road, riding steadily through San Giovanni, past the street where she lived. In her head she said good-bye to the few belongings she had there: a Bible little read; some photos; a few cheap clothes; a music case with some much-loved pieces.

They found the autovia and she saw the sign to the airport. A few miles short of Fiumicino he turned the Vespa into the drive of a low, modern hotel, found a hidden space in the car park at the rear, stopped and turned off the engine.

She got off the scooter without being asked.

"You did well," the man said simply, staring at her.

"Did I have a choice?"

"If you want to live, no, you don't. Have you already forgotten you are in grave danger?"

She glanced at the scooter. "Is that what you are? A thief?"

He nodded, and she wondered if there was the

slightest of smiles behind the matted, grubby beard. "A thief. That's correct, Felicia. We must go inside now."

He waved the key as they rushed past reception, and went to the first floor where he opened the door and ushered her into his room. It was a suite, elegant and expensive, the kind she had only seen in movies. There were two large suitcases already packed on the floor. The pillows of the bed were covered with scattered chocolates. He picked up a couple and gave them to her. She ate greedily. It was good chocolate, the best. The room, she understood, had been waiting here, empty, running up a bill, perhaps for weeks.

"Do you have a passport with you?" he asked.

"Of course. It is the law."

She showed him.

"I meant the other. You have dual nationality. This is important."

"No." She shook her head forcefully. "I am Polish only. That was an accident of birth."

"A lucky accident," he grumbled, and picked up a briefcase by the side of the bed. The man—she could no longer think of him as a tramp—pulled out a blue document, an American passport.

"Your name now is Joanna Phelps. Your mother was Polish, which explains your accent. You are a student at college in Baltimore. Remember all this."

She didn't take the passport, though she couldn't stop herself staring at the gold eagle on the cover.

"Why?" she asked.

"You know why, Felicia," he replied.

"I don't, really . . ."

His strong hands suddenly held her shoulders, shaking her slender frame. His eyes were fierce and unavoidable.

"What's your name? What's your name?"

"My name is Felicia Kaminski. I am nineteen years old. A citizen of the Polish Republic. I was born . . ."

"Felicia Kaminski is dead," he cut in. "Be careful you don't join her."

Stepping back, he said, "Do not answer the door to anyone. Eat and drink from the mini bar if you need something. I must—" he stared at the grubby clothes, hating them—"do something."

He took new clothes out of one of the cases and disappeared into the bathroom. She looked at the second piece of luggage. It seemed expensive. The label bore the name Joanna Phelps and an address in Baltimore. Felicia opened it and found that it was full of new jeans, skirts, shirts and underwear. They were all the right size, and must have cost more than she earned in an entire month.

When he came out he was wearing a dark business suit with a white shirt and elegant silk red tie. He was no more than 40, handsome, Italian-looking, with a sallow skin, clean shaven, rough and red in places from the razor. He had dark, darting eyes and long hair wet from the shower, slicked back on his head, black mostly, with gray flecks. His face seemed more lined than she felt it ought to be, as if there had been pain somewhere, or illness.

He had a phone in his hand.

"In an hour, Joanna, we will go to Fiumicino," he said. "There will be a ticket waiting for you at the first class Alitalia counter. You show them your passport, check in and go straight to the lounge. I will meet you there. I shall be behind you all the way. Do not stop after immigration. Do not look at me. Do not acknowledge me until we have landed and I approach you."

"Where are we going?"

He considered the question, wondering whether to answer.

"First to New York. Then to Washington. You must know this surely. How else would one get back to where you live from Italy?"

She said nothing.

"Where do you live, Joanna?"

She tugged at the label of the case he had provided for her. "I live at 121 South Fremont Avenue, Baltimore. And you?"

He smiled genuinely. In other circumstances, she might have thought she liked this man.

"That is none of your business."

"Your name is?"

He said nothing, but kept on smiling.

Felicia walked quickly to the second case, before he could stop her, and grasped the label.

It was blank. He laughed at her, and she was unsure whether this was a pleasant sound or a cruel one.

"So what do I call you?" she asked.

A theatrical gesture: He placed a forefinger on his reddened chin, stared at the hotel bedroom ceiling, and said, "For now, you may call me Faust."

3

JAMES GRADY

The jetliner glided out of the night to touch down at Washington's Dulles Airport 29 minutes early and 47 minutes before Harold Middleton killed a cop.

As soon as the plane's wheels grabbed runway, Middleton text-messaged his daughter.

She hadn't answered his calls from Europe, and state, county and city police had been vague about protecting a young couple just because a frantic father called from Poland. The D.C. suburban cops seemed skeptical of Middleton's promises that Polish badges and American diplomats would echo his alarm as soon as their chains of command argued out who should contact whom.

Middleton's text-message read: GREEN LANTERN EVAC SCOTLAND.

GREEN LANTERN: His then-wife Sylvia had scoffed at his family code word system to prevent their toddler from being deceived by two-legged predators, but little Charlotte judged the plan cool, especially when Daddy let her make their secret code his (and thus her) favorite comic book hero.

EVAC: Charlotte was nine when the Pentagon Military Intelligence Unit where Middleton spent most of his career ran an evacuation drill. She adopted the word EVAC as a mantra, with significant shifts in irony as she roared through her teenage years.

SCOTLAND: When Charlotte got married, Middleton let her use his suburban house for the wedding's staging ground while he rented another lonely room in a hotel near the Capital Hill garden for the marriage ceremony. Two nights before the wedding, father and daughter got drunk in the hotel bar as she introduced him to a hip single-malt Scotch. From then on, they called that hotel "Scotland."

Told her what to do, thought Middleton. Where to go. That it's really me.

If she got the message.

The seatbelt "ding!" launched Middleton into the plane's aisle. Looping the shoulder strap on his soft black briefcase across his sports jacket kept his hands free. He didn't know where the rest of his luggage was; didn't care. His briefcase held his work, his laptop, iPod and toiletries airport security let him take onto an airplane, plus a paperback copy of Albert Camus's *The Stranger*.

As Middleton was about to reach the plane's door, a couple from first class barged in front of him. The woman, who may have looked great 10 years and a million scowls ago, clutched a battered jewel case to suspiciously firm breasts as she and her sad-eyed husband shuffled up the jet way ahead of Middleton.

Middleton heard the wife huff, "I still can't believe that sister of yours thought she could keep your mother's jewels from me just by going to Europe!"

The husband's flat voice knew its own irrelevance. "We all make mistakes."

They bumbled ahead to Customs, where a surgical-gloved guard carefully examined the jewel box's glittering necklaces, bracelets and earrings, comparing them to a transit document the wife kept tapping with her crimson fingernails. When he was through, the first class couple trudged ahead of Middleton through the terminal.

Middleton's jagged nerves keyed him into a detached hyper-vigilance he'd not felt since returning to the Balkans' slaughterhouse. There, all he had to fear were the ghosts of strangers. Now he felt his own life crawl along the edge of a straight razor.

He smelled his fellow travelers. Damp wool scent of lived-in clothes. Deodorants' metallic perfumes. Stale beer from the Englishman who'd tried to drown his fear of flying.

Middleton heard a child whine, and sobs from a Spec 4 soldier, who was all of 20 years old, as he marched toward a flight to Germany with connections to Iraq. An unseen CD blasted drums and crashing guitars: Middleton recognized Springsteen, and then remembered that expanding his range of classic rock music was the only debt besides Charlotte he owed his ex.

Night filled the terminal windows. Ads landscaped its walls. The musician in Middleton found melody in crowd movements synced with his rhythmic march to a bus for the main terminal. From there, he'd find his car in Long Term Parking, race to Scotland, working his cell phone the whole way. He saw all that with the absolute clarity of what is and what would be.

Looming beyond the shuffling first-class couple, Middleton saw a cop hurrying toward him. Saw the cop's blue uniform. Saw his shoulder-holstered black automatic. Saw a second pistol on the cop's black-leather belt along with handcuffs, ammo pouches, an empty loop for a radio.

They were 10 steps apart when Middleton matched the cop's face to photos he'd seen in Poland of a murderer.

The fake cop unsnapped his hip holster.

Middleton shoved the first-class woman into the pistol-drawing cop.

The fragile jewel case popped out of her grasp and flew toward the cop, who knocked it away. The case burst open. Glittering objects rained on the airport crowd.

First-class woman clawed at the cop: "Mine! Mine!"

Her bumped husband fell into an empty chair.

The fake cop pointed his gun at Middleton's face, as the woman continued to flail at him.

• • •

The gunshot reverberated through the terminal to Gate 67 some 40 feet off to Middleton's left where FBI Agent M. T. Connolly was snapping a handcuff onto her own wrist. The handcuffs' other clamp already circled the wrist of Dan Kohrman, who wore a second set of handcuffs shackling his wrists in front of him. Connolly's close-cropped brass hair came up to the shoulder of the husky Kohrman who'd been apprehended in Chicago on a federal Flight To Avoid Prosecution charge and extradited to D.C. Chicago cops passed him off.

Connolly hadn't needed to double cuff Kohrman. True, he was a felony fugitive, but he'd embezzled funds as a lawyer. Not the kind of bad boy who'd give "14-years-on-the-bricks her" any trouble. No, she cuffed her left hand to his right hand because she didn't feel like talking to the scum-bag. Easier to jerk him where she wanted him to go.

He'd protested his innocence as Windy City cops led him off the plane toward Connolly and a uniformed Virginia state trooper who had been assigned to accompany the FBI during custodial transferals through the state's jurisdiction to a federal lockup. After that . . .

Well, after that, the state trooper had the easy smile of a Dixie scamp. He seemed like a possible diversion from the storm of empty howling in Connolly. His eyes twinkled while they waited for the Chicago plane, indicating to her that he harbored similar thoughts. He introduced himself as George, and she knew he wouldn't be around long enough for her to need to remember his last name.

"Look," Kohrman had said as she clicked her handcuff on his wrist. "Have you asked yourself why I would be so stupid as to steal that money?"

As she tightened the handcuff on her left wrist, Connolly replied, "Like I care about why."

Then she heard the high-caliber pistol shot crackle behind her. Crowd reacting. Trooper George facing the sound source. Screams and she turned, her .40 Glock filling her right hand.

She saw travelers stampeding.

Sensed the taller, trooper-uniformed George draw his gun.

Glimpsed a thick, black-haired American crashing onto a cop.

The roar of the gun in Middleton's face deafened him. The muzzle flash novaed his eyes. But as the bullet cut wide, Middleton fell onto his would-be killer and the crazed woman from first class, and they crashed to the floor. The gun flew from the killer's hand as hordes of airline travelers panicked in a 21st century terrorism nightmare.

Middleton's vision returned. But why can't I hear? Why is there no noise?

He scrambled after a 9mm Beretta gliding silently across a jewel-strewn floor.

The fake cop chopped at the first-class woman's

throat. Jumped to his feet. Reached for his shoulder-holstered second pistol.

Middleton heard only the hammering of his own heart. He grabbed the Beretta and fired at the man who was drawing a second gun.

A glowing green neon Starbucks sign exploded on a wall beyond as the fake cop took a marksman's stance and acquired his target. His black shoes crunched white pearls scattered on the floor.

The fake cop and Middleton fired at the same time.

His arm unsteady, Middleton's bullet missed.

The fake cop's bullet missed too because he slipped on pearls and tumbled back through the air.

Off to Middleton's left, State Trooper George saw a uniformed police officer in trouble. Saw the cop fall. Panicked civilians ran between Trooper George and the gun battle. George glimpsed his target—tapped out two snap shots.

Missed!

Middleton saw a nearby black plastic chair shatter.

Instantly knew why, whirled. His eyes locked on a man wearing a blue uniform like the enemy's. Middleton fired four slugs at that second uniform.

Connolly heard the whine of bullets, the roar of a gun.

As the fugitive Kohrman screamed, Connolly saw Trooper George. Flat on his back, a hole at the collar of the blue-uniformed shirt over his bulletproof vest. A red stream flowed from George's neck. His eyes stared at the ceiling.

Connolly lunged toward the fallen trooper, but Kohrman jerked her handcuffed left arm and she tipped back toward him.

"I wanted to make it big!" screamed Kohrman. "All right? I admit it! Just don't shoot—"

"Shut up!" Connolly shouted as she broke his nose with the butt of her pistol.

Kohrman crumpled, dead weight she dragged to Trooper George bleeding on the floor. Dropped her gun, pressed her free right hand over the gushing hole in the trooper's neck.

"You're going to make it!" she screamed at the fallen officer.

But she knew that was a lie.

Can't hear!

Middleton saw the second uniformed man who'd tried to shoot him crash to the floor. Middleton whirled his deaf attention to the nearby fake cop, who scrambled to his feet on the floor's glittering debris and fled through an emergency exit door.

Get him before he gets me! Or my daughter!

Battling in a world of silence, Middleton saw men and women dive for cover behind waiting room chairs. He saw their muted screaming faces.

First-class husband slumped in a black plastic chair, his face contorted like a laughing clown, staring at the tiled floor where his buxom wife lay gasping for air.

Middleton's eyes followed the husband's focus.

Saw flecks of gold paint on the tiles.

Saw broken shards of red and green and white stones.

Saw glittering glass ground to dust.

Saw a fallen cell phone spinning to a stop amid the rainbow rubble.

Middleton scooped up the cell phone as he burst to the emergency exit, broke out to the night from a facility designed by Homeland Security to prevent people from storming into it and its planes, not to keep people from running away.

Swallowed by cool air, Middleton stood at the top of metal stairs leading to the vast fields of runways where jets taxied, landed, took off—all in terrible silence.

A baggage caravan rolled silently across the dark tarmac. No sign of the fake cop. Middleton suddenly realized he stood spotlighted by the door's white light—a perfect target.

He ran down the stairs. Ran toward the glowing swoop of the main terminal.

A jumbo jet dropped out of the sky, skimmed over his head as he staggered across a runway. He ran under a second airliner as it climbed into the night. The pressure changing wakes of those jet engines popped his gunshot-deafened ears.

Suddenly, blessedly, he heard jet engines roar.

Get to Scotland, he thought. Got to get to Scotland. The strap of his briefcase boa-constrictored his chest as he gasped for oxygen. Sweat stuck his shirt to his skin. His leg muscles burned and felt as if someone smashed a baseball bat into his right kneecap.

He knew better than to try for his car. They—whoever they were—might be waiting for him in the parking garage.

Pistol shoved in the back waistband of his pants, Middleton loped to the front of the main terminal. No one paid much attention—people run through airports all the time. A long line of people stood waiting their turn for a taxi.

To his left, he saw a young couple exiting a Town Car. He burst between them, leapt into the back seat before the driver could protest.

"Go!"

The man behind the wheel stared into the rearview mirror.

"Two-fifty," Middleton said, digging into his pocket for U.S. currency.

He sank into the backseat cushion of the taxi as it shot away from the terminal. "Capitol Hill."

The driver let him out in front of the Supreme Court that glowed like a gray-stone temple across from Congress' white-castle Capitol. Middleton walked through a park and saw no one but the nocturnal outline of a patrolling Capitol Hill policeman and his leashed German shepherd.

Scotland was a hotel built back when visiting Washington wasn't a big business. Middleton passed through the hotel's glass doors, walked straight to the registration desk.

"No sir, no young woman by that name is registered. No Mister and Missus either. No sir, no messages. Yes sir, I'll call you at the bar if anything changes. Oh wait, what was your name? Excuse me: Sir? Sir?"

In the dark lounge, Middleton told the bartender, "Glenfiddich, rocks."

After the ice melted in his drink, Middleton concluded that his daughter wasn't coming. Wasn't here. Wasn't where she was supposed to be.

He laid the cell phone he'd snatched off the floor beside his glass on the bar. A pre-pay. Not his. He fished his phone from his briefcase. Ached to call someone, anyone. But he couldn't risk a monster hacking and tracking his calls. Besides, who could he talk to? Who could he trust now? Maybe killers had infiltrated Uncle Sam's badges too.

Breathe. Breathe.

You're a musician. Be like Beethoven. Hear the full, true symphony.

Do what you do best.

Interpret. Authenticate.

Whatever this was started in Europe. Could still be evolving there with other assassins, other terrors. Started way back with Kosovo, a war criminal, and a phantom mastermind. Was worth killing for. Worth dying for.

From Poland, the fake cop rode the plane that Middleton was supposed to be on. He might have spotted an airport cop getting off shift, followed him to his parking spot, snapped his neck, stuffed the dead cop in the trunk of his own car, stripped the corpse of clothes, weapons and IDs. As a cop in uniform, the killer strolled into the airport to meet every plane from Paris.

But who were his partners?

Focus on what makes sense.

I know something. Or someone. That's why they wanted to kill me. I have something that somebody wants. Or am something. I did something.

But the truth is, I'm not that important.

Wasn't. Am now.

That new truth is calibrated in blood.

In his mind, Middleton heard random notes, not a symphony. He flashed on jazz. When asked how a musician could slip into a free form jam that he'd neither started nor would finish, legendary pianist Night Train Jones said: "You gotta play with both hands."

Middleton put his cell phone inside his shirt pocket.

Stared at the cell phone he'd found spinning on the floor in a combat zone.

The phone had been turned on when Middleton grabbed it. If someone could locate a cell phone just because it was turned on, they were already rocketing toward him. Middleton found the "recent calls" screen. On the inside front cover of the paperback Camus novel, Middleton wrote the phone number that this cell phone had connected to for 3 minutes and 19 seconds. That same number sent this phone one text message:

122 S FREEMNT A BALMORE

Baltimore, thought Middleton. A 40-minute drive from this bar stool. A train ride from Union Station kitty-corner to the hotel. A few blocks north of the train station was a bus depot from which silver boxes roared up Interstate 95 to Charm City where Middleton spent a lot of time at the Peabody Conservatory of Music.

Middleton wrote the address inside the novel's cover.

He went to the men's room and, in the clammy locked stall, counted his remaining cash: $515 American, $122 in Euros. Credit cards, but the second he used one to buy a ticket, meal or motel, he would pop up on the grid. He checked the ammo magazine in his scavenged Beretta: eight bullets.

Can go a long way and nowhere at all on what I've got, thought Harold Middleton.

Back on the bar stool, he realized he reeked of frenzy. The bar mirror made him flinch. He looked terrible. Burned out and all but buried. Worse, he looked memorable.

Middleton left enough cash on the bar, walked toward the night.

He turned away from well-lit streets, still not ready to risk a phone call or a train or a bus or shelter for the night. Walked past empty office buildings.

Out of the darkness loomed a man brandishing a butcher knife.

Middleton froze two paces from a blade that would've punctured his throat.

Butcher-knife man growled: "Give it up! Cash. Wallet. Hurry!"

So Middleton reached under his gray sports jacket and came out with Beretta steel.

"Go, baby!" yelled the robber to a waiting car. He dropped the knife.

"Freeze, baby," Middleton shouted, "or I'll blow his head off, then kill you too!"

Middleton kept the robber in his vision while turned toward the rusted car idling at the curb, its front passenger door gaping open like the maw of a shark.

Never heard it roll up behind me. Never saw it coming. Wake up!

The robber said: "We want a lawyer!"

Middleton jerked his head toward the open car door—but kept his gun locked on the robber. "Get in and you might get out of this alive."

The hands-high scruffy man eased into the shotgun seat of the idling car. Middleton slid into the backseat behind him, told the boney young woman with blazing eyes behind the steering wheel, "Do what I say or I'll blast a bullet in your spine."

"Baby!" yelled her partner. "You were supposed to beat it outta trouble!"

Not anger, thought Middleton, that's not the music. More a plea. And sorrow.

"Fool! He'd have lit you up! Word, Marcus: I ain't never gonna leave you go."

"Knew you weren't meant for no thug life." Notes of pride. Sorrow.

"Where?" the woman asked the dark silhouette in her rearview mirror.

"We're going to Baltimore," Middleton said. "Drive."

4

S. J. ROZAN

Swift and silent as a cheetah after an antelope, the dust cloud chased the approaching Jeep. Almost, you could imagine it putting on a burst of speed, catching the Jeep and devouring it. Squinting over the sun-baked soil, Leonora Tesla gave in to an ironic smile as she found herself rooting for the dust.

Since she'd come to Namibia she'd seen this contest often, the predator running the prey. Conscientiously, she told herself not to take sides—they were all God's creatures, and they all had to eat—but her heart was always with the prey. And her heart was usually broken, because the predator usually won. Now she was on the other side, but—as usual, Leonora!—in a hopeless cause. The dust would lose this race, settling into defeat as the Jeep came to a stop in front of her hut.

At least this time, she wouldn't have to worry about heartbreak: This would not be a life-and-death struggle, only an annoyance in her day.

"He's a funder," her program manager had said over the village's single crackling telephone, calling from Windhoek, his voice equal amounts sympathy and command. "You will have to see him."

Leonora Tesla had come to the bush so she wouldn't have to see anyone, except the HIV-positive women she worked with. After The Hague, after the hunting—after the shock of being called together and told by Harold the Volunteers must disband—even the smaller African cities had been too much for her. So she'd gone to the bush, traveling from village to village, staying not long in any one place. Her mandate was to establish craft cooperatives, micro-financing women's paths to independence. The work suited her. Her days were filled now with distracting minutiae—finding hinges in one village so another's kiln door could be repaired; lending the equivalent of four American dollars so a group could buy paper on which to keep records of baskets sold. And with beauty: the color-block quilts, the Oombiga pots whose tradition had almost been lost. Beauty suited Tesla too. Visual beauty: the way the women weaved echoed the stark subtlety of the African landscape. And musical beauty: The only artifact of 21st century technology she'd brought into the bush was an iPod loaded with—among other things—Bach preludes, Shostakovich symphonies and Beethoven sonatas. Reluctantly, she removed it now, cutting off Chopin as the Jeep neared. She hoped this wouldn't take long. She'd ferry him around, this funder from . . . She'd forgotten to ask. She'd show him the kiln, the looms, the workshop. She'd rattle off her statistics on life-span extension and self-sufficiency, give him her little speech about hope for the next generation. The women would present him with a quilt or a pot for which he could have no possible use and he'd be patronizingly pleased with them and inordinately proud of himself for making this all possible. Then maybe he'd go away and leave them in peace.

Oh, Leonora, at least try to smile.

The other Volunteers used to say that regularly, and precisely because their work gave them little to smile about, she'd try. She did it now, a polite smile for the angular blond man who stepped from the Jeep. He smiled back and slapped his hat against his thigh to shake off the dust. He took off his sunglasses: well trained in the art of courtesy, at least.

"Leonora Tesla? I'm Günter Schmidt."

He spoke in English with a soft accent she couldn't quite place. Not German, but no law said his German name meant he was brought up in that country. That's what the permeability of European borders was about. It was supposed to be a good thing.

They shook hands. Schmidt's was soft and fleshy, as befit someone who dispensed money from behind a desk. "You've had a long drive," she said. "Sit down. I'll get you something to drink." She indicated a stool on the hard clay under the overhang, but he followed her into the house. He'd learn, she thought. In Africa the indoor, though shadowed and appealing, was never cooler than outside.

Still smiling, Schmidt dropped himself onto one of the rough-hewn chairs at her plank table. She handed him a bottle of BB orange soda. In a hut without electricity, of course she had no refrigerator, but she'd learned the African trick of burying bottles in a box in the hut's clay floor, so the drink was relatively cool. "We'll be more comfortable outside," she suggested, resigned to try to be pleasant to this intruder.

"No," he said, "I'd rather stay here. Leonora."

She bristled at the odd way he said her name, but his expression was mild as he looked about her hut. So she shrugged, wiped her brow with her kerchief and sat beside him.

"You've lived here long?" Schmidt asked, taking a pull from his soda bottle.

"No. I don't live anywhere long. My work takes me many places."

"That would account for the . . . simplicity."

"And yet my possessions, few as they are, are more numerous than those of the women in our programs. When you're rested, I'll take you to see the kiln. We'll be covering a lot of ground today if you want to see the full scope of our work." She stood to reach her own Jeep keys on the hook by the door.

"No, I think we'll stay here. Leonora."

She turned sharply. His smile and the mild

expression in his eyes were still in place, but his hand held a pistol, pointed at her.

Calm, Leonora. Stay calm. "What do you want?"

"Where is Harold Middleton?"

Tesla's heart, already pounding, gave a lurch. But she spoke calmly. "Harold? How would I possibly know?"

Schmidt didn't answer her. The gun moved slightly, as though seeking a better angle.

"Isn't he in America, in Washington? That's where he lives."

"If he were in Washington," Schmidt asked reasonably, "would I be here?"

"Well, I haven't heard from him in almost a year."

"I don't know whether that's true, though eventually I'm sure I'll find out. But it doesn't matter. Whether you've heard from him or not, you know where he'd go. If, say, he were in trouble."

In trouble? "No, I don't."

"When you worked together—"

"When we did, I might have been able to tell you. But I don't know anything about his life now. He teaches music; I don't even know where."

Neither of them had moved since Tesla had seen the pistol. Neither of them moved now, in the stretching silence. A breeze rustled the leaves in the acacia behind the hut. Sweat trickled down Tesla's spine.

"Who are you? What do you want with Harold?"

He laughed. "I suppose you had to ask that, but you know I won't tell you. But it's about your work, Leonora."

"The Volunteers?"

His smile was bitter. "Your work. So. You really don't know where Middleton is? Not even if I shoot you?"

A gunshot roar ricocheted off the tin roof and mud walls; Tesla stumbled, grasped the plank table for support as clay shards flew everywhere. She found herself staring into Schmidt's mild eyes. Wheezing a few breaths, quieting her heart by an act of will, she answered him.

"Even if you shoot me. I don't know."

Schmidt nodded. "All right. You don't know where he'd go if he were in trouble. I suppose then we'll have to depend on what he'd do, if you were in trouble." He stood. "Come."

"What?"

"As you said: We'll be covering a lot of ground."

She walked ahead of the gun out onto the uneven baked earth. The glaring sunlight was unforgiving; she did not turn, but waited. There: a stutter in his step, a whisper of plastic on fabric. Behind her, Schmidt reached into his pocket for his sunglasses, she dropped down and rolled into him. He stumbled; she yanked his ankle forward, threw her weight sideways into his other knee. Dust boiled as he thudded to the ground. Another shot screamed, but out here in the endless bush it didn't thunder, and she'd been prepared to hear it. The gun waved wildly, looking for her, but by the second shot she was in the hut and by the third she'd hurled a clay pot with the force and accuracy of Yaa Asantewa's spear.

In the whirling dust, Schmidt—and more important, the gun—was still.

Forcing her breathing even, Tesla crouched by the door, waiting. When all had been motionless for a full minute, she crept to the table, reached down for one of the soda bottles and flung it at Schmidt's head. On impact it smashed into glittering shards, but Schmidt didn't move.

Slowly, she rose. She made her way to where Schmidt lay in the settling dust. His blood trickled into the dry soil amid the shards of a once-beautiful pot. There, you see, Leonora? This time you were on the side of the dust. And the predator always wins.

Her first steps back inside took her to the plastic water bucket in her makeshift sink. She scooped with her hands, splashed water over her face and head as though here, at the edge of the Namib, water was hers to waste.

Then she made her way swiftly about the room, collecting the few things she would take. When her canvas bag was packed she used a knife to slit the seam she'd sewed on the thin mattress as she had on each mattress in each hut she'd stayed in. She extracted the envelope of American dollars and the small, battered portfolio she'd had with her since

The Hague. She slipped them both into the side pocket with the iPod, zipped and she was done.

Getting Schmidt into the Jeep was harder. She was strong but he was tall, and leverage was a problem. Eventually, his head wrapped in a towel to keep bloodstains from the seat, she'd maneuvered him into the back, fished the keys from his pocket and started the engine. Driving along the dust track the way Schmidt had come, she saw ahead the spot she'd been thinking of, where the edge of the road fell off steeply toward the wadi. She passed it and turned around so the Jeep was headed toward her hut. Then, on the curve, she yanked the wheel sharply, opened the door and jumped.

Anywhere in the wadi would have worked, but her luck was better than she'd had the nerve to hope, and the Jeep smacked head-on into an acacia tree. When she reached it—limping slightly, she'd banged her knee—cracks spider-webbed the windshield. Excellent. Then came more sweat, strain and maneuvering, and finally Schmidt was half-in, half-out of the driver's seat. Though the crack in his skull was clearly not from this crash, he was unlikely to be found for a while—except by the hyenas that skulked along this dry streambed. Once they were through, no one would doubt what had killed Günter Schmidt.

Or whoever he was. And wherever he'd come from.

She walked back to the hut, hoping she could

walk out the ache in her knee. Once there, she stripped and washed in the little water she'd left herself. She changed clothes, took what she'd been wearing and the bloody towel in a pillowcase. Slinging it and her bag into her own Jeep, Tesla paused. Though she'd lived in and left too many places to make a habit of goodbyes, she took a moment to stare at the hut, and then turned to salute the wide brown land. She'd thought this might be home, but now she doubted she'd be back.

The drive to Windhoek Airport took a little more than three hours. Once there, she used all four of her credit cards to withdraw as much cash as she could. With what she'd taken from the mattress, she'd be all right for a while. On one of the cards she bought a ticket on the connecting flight through Munich to Washington, D.C. Then she exited the terminal and boarded the long-distance bus to Cape Town.

She didn't know if her credit cards were being monitored, but she had to take the possibility into account. In Cape Town, she'd buy a ticket in cash.

To New York.

Where you could catch a train to Washington, Harold had told her, a dozen times a day.

Hugging her bag to her, feeling the portfolio's stiffness through the canvas, Leonora stared out the window at the dry land, the lonesome trees.

A dozen trains a day.

That ought to be enough.

5

ERICA SPINDLER

Charlotte Middleton-Perez cracked open her eyes, disoriented. Not home. Not the dining room at the Ritz.

Bright, antiseptic white. Shiny surfaces, stiff sheets. She hurt. Ached everywhere, especially her lower back.

The squeak and rattle of a cart broke the silence. Muffled voices followed. She shifted her gaze. Her husband Jack by the bed, head in hands. The picture of grief.

With a shattering sense of loss, she remembered: standing up. Seeing the blood. Crying out, then gasping as pain knifed through her belly.

She brought a hand to her abdomen, vision blurring with tears. She'd had a life growing inside her. A baby boy. She and Jack had begun picking out names.

Had. Past tense. Now, no life inside her. No little boy with Jack's blue eyes and her dark hair.

Her tears spilled over, rolling down her cheeks, hot and bitter.

He lifted his head. His eyes were red-rimmed from crying.

"Charley," he said.

The one word conveyed a world of emotion—

despair and regret, love and need. For comfort. To understand—how could this have happened?

They'd reached the second trimester. Safe, they'd thought. Out of the woods. Common wisdom validated their belief.

Her fault? Working too hard? Not enough rest?

As if reading her thoughts, Perez stretched out a hand. She took it and he curled his fingers protectively around hers. "Not your fault, Charley. The doctor said these things . . . happen."

She shook her head. "That's not good enough. I need to know why."

He cleared his throat. "They're going to run some tests. On us. On our . . . The miscarriage. He suggested an ultrasound of your uterus, an x-ray, too."

She squeezed her eyes shut as he tightened his fingers on hers. "This is a setback. It really hurts, but we'll have—"

"No."

"—other childre—"

"Don't. Please." Her voice cracked. "I wanted this baby . . . I—I already loved him."

"I understand," he said with apparent sympathy.

And he always seemed to. She didn't know what she had done to deserve his love. They'd met at Tulane University in New Orleans. She had been stunned when he asked her out, when he pursued her. She wasn't an extraordinary beauty. Just pleasant looking—average face, average figure.

And Jack was off the charts handsome. Smart. Educated. From an influential Louisiana family. His falling for her had been as much a mystery as a miracle.

"Have you heard from Harry?" she asked. She'd stopped calling her father Dad on her thirteenth birthday. She was Charley, he was Harry and her mother was perpetually horrified by the both of them.

"Not yet."

"You left a message—"

"At the restaurant. And just a bit ago on his cell phone. It went automatically to voicemail."

He was delayed, still in transit. "You didn't tell him—"

He squeezed her fingers again. "Just that we were here. To call on my cell. I left my number."

She swallowed past the sudden rush of tears. "Mother?" she managed.

"No answer, home or cell."

"Ms. Middleton?"

They turned. Two men stood in the doorway, expressions solemn. Both men, dressed in dark suits, were pin neat and pressed, despite the hour. She wasn't surprised when they introduced themselves as federal officers. "We need to ask you a few questions."

"Now?" Perez asked as he stood. "Here?"

"It's about your father," the taller of the two said, producing his Department of Justice ID.

"About Harry?"

"Harold Middleton, yes. When's the last time you spoke with him?"

The hair on the back of her neck prickled. "Before he left for Europe. A week or so before."

"Did he seem himself?"

"Yes. But why—"

"Did he express any concerns about the trip? Any anxiety? Unexpected excitement?"

"My father was a seasoned traveler, Agent—"

"Smith," he offered. "Did you get the sense this trip was different from others he's taken?"

"None at all."

"You planned to meet last evening? At the Ritz dining room?"

"Yes . . . But how—" She didn't finish the thought. The feds could find out anything. Harry had taught her that. "For a late supper. I didn't make it."

Her throat closed over the words. The agents seemed unmoved by her pain. "We're sorry for your loss, Ms. Middleton, but—"

"Mrs. Perez," her husband corrected, voice tight. "As I said, this is not a good time. Either tell us why you're here or leave."

Agent Smith looked Perez in the eyes. "Perez is a well known name down in Louisiana."

Perez frowned. "Meaning what?"

"It's a name we're familiar with, that's all."

Jack August Perez. His family, descendants of

the original Spaniards that settled the New Orleans area, wielded both political and economic influence. In the era of Huey P. Long, they had exerted that power with an iron fist, nowadays with business savvy and brilliant connections.

Angry color stained Perez's cheeks. "What are you getting at?"

Don't let him get to you, she thought. Emotions lead to mistakes. Ones that could prove deadly. Another of Harry's pearls.

What the hell was going on?

She touched her husband's clenched hand. "It's all right, sweetheart. It's just a couple of questions."

"Thank you, Mrs. Perez. Has your father contacted you in the past twenty-four hours?"

"No. I expect his flight was delayed. I'm used to that sort of thing with Harry."

At her response, she felt her husband's startled glance. She didn't acknowledge it. "How did you know I was here, Agent Smith?"

He ignored the question. "I'm afraid your father's in some trouble."

She noticed that while Agent Smith spoke, his partner studied her reactions. She also noticed that every so often he rubbed the back of his hand against his leg, as if scratching at a bite or wiping at a stain.

Most un-fed like. Feds were trained to be as robotic as possible. Nervous twitches were not an option.

"Trouble? I don't understand."

"He was questioned in Warsaw concerning three murders in Europe."

"Harry?" That incredulous retort came from Perez. "You have the wrong Harold Middleton."

The agent's gaze flickered to Perez, then settled on her once more. "Your father was able to catch an Air France flight out of Paris several hours later. He arrived at Dulles—then he shot and killed a police officer."

She who couldn't hold back. "Impossible!"

"I'm sorry."

"That's not my father."

"I understand how you must feel. It's a shock, but we have witnesses—"

"My father couldn't have shot anybody. First off, Harold Middleton has spent his life fighting for what's right. Hunting down and bringing to justice the sorts of monsters who terrorize and murder. That said, where did he get a gun? He'd just gotten off an international flight. Who was this cop? Why would my father want to kill him?"

She held his gaze; the tense silence crackled between them. After a moment, the agent broke the contact, inclined his head. "Those are all questions only your father can answer. We need to speak with him."

The last thing she was about to do was help them find Harry.

The Feds were like buzzards on road kill—once

they made up their mind someone was guilty, they'd move heaven and earth to "prove" it.

"What can I do?" she asked, sounding annoyingly earnest to her own ears.

"Let us know the minute you hear from him." Agent Smith handed her his card. She gazed down at it, adorned with the Bureau's familiar red, white, blue and gold seal.

He handed one to Perez. "That's my cell number. Call anytime, day or night."

"I will." She ran her thumb across the business card, heart pounding. "And if you find him—"

"You'll be the first to know."

"This is all a mistake. You're looking for the wrong man."

"For your sake, I hope so." As the two crossed to the door, Smith turned, meeting her gaze once more. Something in his expression made her skin crawl. "Thank you for your cooperation."

The moment the door shut behind them, she swung her legs over the side of the bed. "We're getting out of here. Now."

"Charley, what—"

"This whole thing stinks. And I'm going to find out wh—" She stood and a wave of dizziness swept over her.

Perez grabbed her arm, steadying her. "Harry's in some trouble, no doubt. But there's nothing you can do about it right now—and certainly not in your condition. I'll get the nurse to call Doctor

Levine and find out when you're being released, and we'll plan from there."

She shook off his hand. "You don't get it. I'm not going to lie around here and do nothing when I know Harry's in danger."

"For God's sake, Charley. You're in more danger than he is. You just had a miscarriage. Doctor Levine said to expect discomfort and bleeding. That you'd be weak. He advised taking it easy for a couple days. I'm not letting you walk out of here without his okay."

"Try to stop me." She took a deep breath and looked her husband squarely in the eyes. "Those guys weren't FBI."

Without waiting for a response, she crossed to the room's version of a closet, a press board armoire. Her panties and trousers were blood-stained. The panties were ruined, she decided, so she would have to make do with the pads the hospital had provided. If she tied her jacket around her waist, her dark-colored trousers would do until she could replace them.

She glanced at her husband as he watched her. "Those cards 'Agent Smith' handed us were bogus," she said. "Take a good look. Cheap stock. Laser jet printing. Run your finger over it. The Bureau's cards are engraved. This one could've been printed from any home computer."

She stepped into the stained trousers, a lump in her throat. She swallowed past it. There would be a lifetime to mourn their loss. Right now, Harry needed her.

"The only number on Smith's card," she continued, "is a cell number."

Perez frowned, struggling to come to grips with what she was proposing. "So where's the Bureau's number?"

"Exactly."

He rubbed the bridge of his nose. "Charley, have you considered that you might be a little emotionally unstable right now? You've suffered a loss . . . It's been a shock. I think taking a step back and a deep breath might be a good idea. I'll check you out, we'll go home. See if Harry's there or left us a message. You need a change of clothes, something to eat. We'll sort everything out."

"Do you trust me?"

"Of course."

"Then help me. Please."

In the end, she wore him down. Worried that one of the bogus agents was watching the front of the hospital, she refused to allow him to officially check her out. The hospital would insist on a wheelchair—standard policy—and a front-door exit. Instead they took the stairs and slipped out the delivery entrance.

She waited while he brought the car around. Once they were both buckled in, he looked at her. "What's the plan?"

"We find Harry."

He smiled at her. "Good plan. How do y—"

The faint sound of a digitized version of the song "Brown-Eyed Girl" interrupted him.

Her cell phone's ring tone.

"It's in your purse," he said. "I locked it in the—"

"Trunk."

He shifted into park, threw open his car door and climbed out. A moment later he returned with her purse, cell clipped to it, message light blinking frantically.

A number she didn't recognize—perhaps her father had bought a prepaid for security. She quickly scrolled through a half-dozen missed calls and one text message waiting. All from Harry.

She returned the last call first, and it was answered on the first ring. "Dad, it's me. Thank God! I was so worried."

"Charlotte! Where are you?"

"Jack and I—"

She bit the words back, realization crashing in on her. Not her father. Her father hadn't called her Charlotte since the second grade.

"Charlotte? Sweetheart, are you—"

With a sound of distress, she hung up. "Drive, Jack. Now."

He did as she instructed. "What happened?"

"Someone pretended to be Harry. They wanted to know where I was."

"Check your messages."

She did. At the sound of her father's voice relief flooded her.

"Charley, I've been delayed. I hope to still make a late dinner. Love you."

She frowned at the second message. "Charley, there's a situation here. I'll explain everything when I get there. Look . . . Be careful. Stay with Jack. Don't trust anyone you don't know. My flight's due into Dulles at 7:10 p.m."

By the third and last message there was no denying the panic in his voice. "Where are you? I'm boarding the Paris flight. When you get this, dial back so I'll know you're okay."

She checked the text message next.

GREEN LANTERN EVAC SCOTLAND

She stared at those four little words, feeling as if all the air had suddenly been sucked out of the car's interior.

"What's wrong?"

"Change in plans. We're going to Capitol Hill. The Scotland—The St. Regis."

While he drove, she explained about the code. When she finished, he glanced at her. "This is a gag?"

"Hardly. Harry would never have sent that text message unless it was for real."

"Maybe he didn't send it?"

The thought chilled her, but only for a moment. "No, no one else would know our code. Even mother only knew part of it. Harry sent it."

"This makes no sense. It's like some cloak-and-dagger parlor game. Only you're telling me it's real." Perez pulled up in front of the hotel. "What is your dad, some kind of a spy?"

She flung open the car door. "Wait here. I'll be right back."

Moments later, she greeted the guest services agent. She dug a photo of Harry out of her wallet; the guy at the desk squinted at it, then nodded.

"He was here. Looking for some woman. You, I suppose. Went to the bar to wait."

She thanked him and hurried to the lounge. She saw right away that he wasn't there.

She crossed to the bar. The bartender was busy with another patron, a stunning redhead. While she waited for him to finish, her attention was drawn to the television behind the bar, the news story being broadcast. A shooting at Dulles. A police officer down. The grainy image of the suspect.

Harry. It couldn't be true.

"What can I get you?"

She looked at the bartender. She had the photo of her father out, ready to ask if the man had seen him, if he knew where he'd gone. Instead, she shook her head and slipped the photo back into her pocket. She couldn't chance him recognizing Harry and sounding the alarm.

"Nothing. I just remembered . . . Sorry."

She turned and quickly left, aware of the bartender's gaze on her. As she strode past the desk again, she glanced the attendant's way. He was on the phone; when he saw her looking his way, he quickly averted his eyes.

If those goons had what they wanted, they wouldn't have paid her the little visit in the hospital. That was the good news.

The bad news. Harry was wanted in connection with the murder of a cop. That part of the "agent's" story had been legitimate.

By now, the police knew who he was, where he worked and lived. Where she lived. They were amassing the names of friends and coworkers. He wouldn't be able to use his credit cards or cell phone. His car would be off-limits, as would his home.

He had two groups after him—the fake police and the real ones.

Her husband was waiting for her at the hotel entrance, expression tight. "Any luck?"

"He was here. He's not now."

"Look, I was listening to the news and—"

"I know," she said, cutting him off. "I saw it on the TV. In the bar."

They hurried up the block to their BMW and slid inside. "Maybe those guys were real agents?"

"No way," she replied. "Mother lives close by. Maybe she's heard from him."

"Sylvia and your father hate each other."

Hate was a strong word, but she certainly wouldn't call them friends. A more mismatched union she couldn't imagine. Plus, her mother had never forgiven Harry for Charlotte liking him more than her. And for turning her only child into what she called a "do-gooder, spy-in-training."

The marriage's final straw had been the brief affair he'd had with one of his fellow Volunteers— Leonora Tesla.

"Let's try there anyway. At the very least, I can borrow a change of clothes."

Her mother would ask about the baby. They'd have to explain. She brought a hand to her empty belly. She didn't want to talk about it. She couldn't.

Falling apart was a luxury she couldn't afford right now.

They made her mother's upscale Georgetown neighborhood in less than 20 minutes. Easing to a stop in front of the two-story colonial, they climbed out of the car and hurried up the walk.

Her mother's Mercedes sedan was parked in the drive. The porch was dark, though light glowed in several of the windows.

Charley rang the bell. From inside came the frenzied yapping of Bella, her mother's Pomeranian.

"Mother!" she called, ringing again. "It's me!"

Maybe she'd gone out with a friend who had picked her up. Or she was on a date.

No. This wasn't right. She felt it in her gut.

Beside her, Perez dialed his mother-in-law's number. It rang twice, four times, six times.

Heart thundering, she dug in her purse for her key ring. She kept one of her mother's spares in case of emergency. She found it, fitted the key in the lock and eased the door open.

"Mom!" she called. Bella came running from the kitchen, across her mother's bright white carpeting. Leaving a trail of perfect little paw prints.

Red prints.

A cry slipped past her lips. With an order for her to "stay put," Perez started for the kitchen. She followed.

They stopped at the kitchen entry. Her mother lay on the tile floor. Face up, eyes open. Vacant. Seeping blood had formed wing shapes on either side of her torso. Bella had run around and around her mistress, through the blood, creating a bizarre, almost floral pattern on the white tile.

Her mother had been dressed for bed. She wore a teal-colored silk robe. The robe's flap had fallen open, exposing her legs and an edge of lacy lingerie. One hand rested on her chest, as if she had grabbed at her heart, the other at her side.

"Oh Mother." Whimpering, she took a step forward, then stopped, lightheaded, and grasped the counter for support.

Her husband inched toward his mother-in-law's body, careful to avoid the blood. He squatted and checked her pulse.

Struggling to come to grips with what had happened, she shifted her gaze. It landed on an item peeking out from under the cabinet. She blinked, focusing. A candy-bar wrapper. With the toe of her shoe, she nudged it out. Milka, a European brand, one difficult to acquire in the states. She tilted her head. This one was from Poland.

She stared at it, blood thundering in her head. Her father's favorite chocolate. His secret passion. One that they shared.

"She's dead, Charley."

"We've got to get out of here. Now." She snatched up the candy wrapper and stuffed it into her pocket.

"What are you doing? Charley, that could be evidence. We've got to call the police."

"They're going to try to pin this on Harry."

"Have you thought that maybe he did—"

"Never, not Dad. He sent me that text message because I'm in danger too. Mother was as well. I don't know why this is happening, but I trust him."

"With your life? With mine as well?"

"Yes." She pressed her lips together as the full meaning of what was happening set in. "We've got to find him."

"How?" Perez dragged a shaking hand through his hair. "We're not wanted by the police, but I'm sure they're looking for us."

She looked back at her mother, fighting back despair—and the urge to crawl into her husband's arms and sob. She was Harold Middleton's daughter. She would hunt down whoever had done this. And make him—or her—pay.

In the distance came the sound of sirens. "The lake house," she said, starting for her mother's bedroom and a change of clothes. "Eventually, Harry will look for us there."

6

JOHN RAMSEY MILLER

In the Dulles parking lot, FBI Agent In Charge M. T. Connolly watched homicide detectives process a policeman's corpse. A deep ligature mark around the murdered cop's neck and blossoms of red in the white of his eyes made cause of death obvious, the same way the security videos made just as obvious the identity of the man who killed him, stole his uniform and stuffed him into the back of a Jeep, where he now lay.

The detectives had arrived in response to the shooting of a state trooper in the concourse. Despite early reports to the contrary, Trooper George was still alive, but in grave condition. Three bullets had deformed against his bulletproof vest and one had gone high and deflected against the collar and severed an artery. He wasn't expected to live. If he did, he could have serious brain damage from blood loss.

Accompanied by homicide detectives, Connolly had gone from the parking deck to the security offices to view the video surveillance. She got a good look at the fake cop who'd fired at the passenger identified by customs as Harold Middleton. Middleton had taken away the assailant's gun and subsequently fired in self-defense. Trooper George assumed the cop was in the right and his target a felon—an understandable mistake. Initially, she had jumped to the same conclusion in the melee, but she had been shackled to her idiot prisoner and couldn't give pursuit until it was too late. She'd assumed that the fake cop had chased Middleton to capture him, but it was now clear he'd run away from her and other security officers who'd come rushing at the sound of gunfire on the concourse. It was also apparent that the fake cop had drawn his gun on Middleton right after Middleton seemed to recognize him.

After Middleton captured the Beretta and used it to defend himself from the trooper's gunfire, he'd fled through an emergency door. The fake cop, wearing the purloined and somewhat ill-fitting uniform, had vanished as had Middleton.

Her next reaction had been to use Bureau resources to find out all she could about Middleton and the cop killer. She and the detectives had agreed that Middleton would be identified only as a material witness who had to be picked up immediately for his own protection. Unless the uniformed cop-killer got to him first. His description was circulated immediately to area law enforcement—picture to follow as soon as it could be printed from the surveillance video—and he was identified as a wanted cop-killer, which meant he'd only live through his apprehension if they found him naked and lying face down on the pavement in front of live TV film crews.

The airport terminal and parking deck teemed with angry cops, crime-scene evidence staff and passenger witnesses. State troopers with dogs were beginning a search of the airport, hoping to find the killer and Middleton, but Connolly doubted they were still in the area. While the cops were reacting like disturbed fire ants, Connolly was working the steps calmly—something that came naturally to her.

She had found a business card lying on the concourse floor, which the detectives had taken as evidence. They didn't know where the card had come from, or if it had meaning to the case, until in watching the video of the struggle between Middleton and the fake cop in slow motion, the card was seen falling to the floor after Middleton's shirt pocket ripped. It read "Jozef Padlo, Deputy Inspector of the Polish National Police."

It caught her like a hammer blow, and, if she hadn't believed in coincidences before, she was a devotee now. Mere minutes later, certainly hours before the detectives would get around to it, Connolly called the phone number and, since it was six hours later in Poland, left the inspector a message on his office voice mail to call her ASAP. Next she tried a number that wasn't on the card, but was in her cell phone, but again Padlo didn't answer. When the inspector's voice mail kicked in, she left the same message. This time she gave Harold Middleton's name figuring that if hearing her voice wasn't enough to get him to respond immediately, Middleton's name would.

When Padlo returned the call 25 minutes later, Connolly had already learned about retired Colonel Harold Middleton from the FBI's Intel group, and decided she was going to work the case come flood or tall cotton. Middleton had located the butcher, KLA's Colonel Agim Rugova, and brought him to trial at The Hague. Rugova had been murdered, so the possibility that the two events were connected thrilled her. Aside from terrorism, there was nothing sexier or better for a career than an international case. And she knew Padlo would cooperate fully with her.

Connolly met Padlo at Quantico three years earlier when he was a guest at the Bureau's law-enforcement classes offered to leading European investigators. As fortune would have it, Connolly had been one of the instructors, and she and Padlo had become close—very close. An image of a naked Padlo sitting cross-legged on her bed—a glass of wine in one hand and a cigarette in the other—as he told her in depth about a cold case he couldn't solve brought a warm smile to her lips.

Jozef Padlo wasn't especially handsome, but there was something about the lanky Pole that strengthened his appearance and negated his well-worn clothes. Connolly knew she wasn't a beauty either, but Padlo saw her as one. He was quick-witted, honest, intelligent, dedicated to his work, spoke fluent English, had big sad eyes, delicate hands and was an attentive lover. For the first time in her life, she hadn't minded the clouds of cigarette smoke. In the intervening years, they spent a few days vacationing together and spoke by telephone two or three times a week. Since both were dedicated to their careers, being together full time was impossible.

Connolly knew she was going to run the case—a cap-feather generator, probably an international one—and if the detectives got in her way, she'd sweep them aside. After all, she'd witnessed the shootout, connected Middleton to the ICCY and kept the cops from misinterpreting Middleton's actions and, possibly, killing him. And she had a working relationship with the foreign authorities. Plus it didn't hurt that she was the southern belle apple of the her boss's eye—they were both from Mississippi and, more important, she had a high-profile case closure rate second to none. It also helped that she never failed to give her superiors as much of the credit as possible.

Connolly looked across the security room at her annoying prisoner, whose wrist was now cuffed to a pipe. EMS had bandaged his nose and cleaned the blood from his face. To turn him over for processing, she'd been calling the U.S. Marshals

Service every 10 minutes for an hour. Finally, she thought, as her phone rang. A callback.

"This is Connolly," she said. "Where the hell are my Marshals?"

"When and where did you last see them?" the Polish inspector asked.

"Well, hello, Inspector Padlo," she answered, softening her voice as she stepped outside.

"Hello, FBI Special Agent Buttercup," Padlo said. "Have you found Middleton?"

"Here's the deal," she said—and told him everything she knew. Padlo listened without interrupting.

When she was finished, he said, "Harold Middleton was the last person to meet with Henryk Jedynak, a collector of old music manuscripts who, along with two witnesses, was murdered here. I had Colonel Middleton picked up and I questioned him. From your description of his assailant, he could be Dragan Stefanovic. I made the Rugova connection to Middleton and showed him an array of photographs of men known to have associated with Rugova in the old days, displaced mercenaries who are now thugs for hire. Stefanovic's picture was among them, as was a man we know only as The Slav. Middleton said he saw The Slav at the airport—apparently waiting for the same flight to Paris that he was taking. The Slav made it out of Paris before we could get French authorities there. As you know, the French authorities generate more red tape than red wine."

"You don't think Middleton may have been somehow involved with Jedynak's death, do you?"

"No. Harold Middleton is one of the good guys, a devoted family man with firm moral fiber, and a man who has made sacrifices so he could right terrible wrongs. Now we have the death of Jedynak, the attempt on Middleton in public and the disappearance of Jedynak's niece."

"His niece. Is it related to his murder?"

"She is a talented violinist so I suspect all of this might be connected to something all three have in common—music. For Middleton and Jedynak, the link runs through rare music manuscripts, which may connect them to Rugova as well."

"Rare music manuscripts . . ."

"As you know, Rugova spent part of the war in Bosnia securing looted treasures from World War II. At St. Sophia, he stole forty-something crates the Nazis had hidden in a sealed chamber: paintings, drawings, golden figures, a few small but valuable bronzes, jewelry—and musical scores. The deaths of almost two hundred civilians got the attention at the time, rightfully so, but Rugova moved those crates. In time, he was eager to trade information on who received the looted art—in exchange for leniency."

"Middleton knew this," Connolly said.

"Middleton had a Chopin manuscript he said might be a fraud, but maybe it is part of this missing collection and he doesn't know it. Or maybe he does. I believed him when I interviewed him and I can tell you that he was suddenly very afraid for his family's welfare. This, I believe, is a valid fear."

Connolly said, "I hope the cop-killer hasn't found him."

"You can be sure that if it's Stefanovic, he isn't working alone," Padlo said. "I can send you photos of the men who served with Rugova. If one of them has killed Middleton, it is to keep the location of the hidden treasure a secret. We're talking millions, maybe even billions of euros here."

"Send the pictures to my email address at the Bureau and I'll send the cop-killer's to you."

"Of course, Buttercup."

She smiled. "You know, Jozef, maybe I can get clearances and have a ticket for you at the airport. I mean, you know these people better than we do, and your assistance could be invaluable."

"Amazingly, I've already told my commissioner that by helping you we can quite possibly help solve Jedynak's murder and bring the killer back here to justice. Maybe you can arrange to have someone meet me at Dulles?"

"I think I can arrange that, Inspector Padlo."

The Slav's name was Vukasin, which meant Wolf, and he was not pleased with how badly things were going. Waiting in a car outside the St. Regis for two of his men, he stiffened at the sight of the elegant woman who had climbed from a cab across the street. She approached his vehicle, opened the door and slid inside.

"Eleana," he said in their native tongue, "your timing is perfect."

"How could I pass up an opportunity to work with dear old friends? And it's Jessica, please."

"Jessica. Very American. Good."

The woman seated beside Vukasin was a Serbian national named Eleana Soberski who was now, thanks to forged documents, a U.S. citizen. Soberski had been a child psychologist before serving as an Intel gatherer assigned to Rugova's forces. The real Jessica Harris had been a volunteer nurse at the central hospital in Belgrade, a woman without close family in the States. She had become eel food in the Danube, compliments of the woman aspiring to steal her identity.

Soberski's primary duty with the KLA during the cleansing action had been interrogating captured enemy soldiers and civilians collected by Rugova's unit. Vukasin, one of Rugova's lieutenants, had seen her work and admired her interrogation methods and enthusiasm. A beauty without a sympathy gene, she rejected the soldiers' overtures and Vukasin came to believe she derived sexual pleasure only when she had utterly terrified people lashed to a table, a chair or hanging from the rafters in excruciating pain.

"Your target is here at this hotel?" she asked.

Vukasin took a picture of two men at a table in a restaurant out of his pocket and handed it to her. "The target is this one—Harold Middleton, who led the Volunteers that tracked Agim and found him."

Her expression hardened. "This is Harold Middleton? I thought he would be more impressive. Where is he?"

"We're not yet sure."

"And you believe he will come here. To a bar. In public."

Vukasin nodded. His ex-wife had been persuaded by his men to list places were Middleton might flee. The St. Regis was one.

"Do you have men inside there?" Harris asked.

"They're on the way." Vukasin smiled. "They're disguised as FBI agents. It will be effective: Middleton is wanted for shooting a policeman at the airport."

"A policeman?"

Vukasin explained.

"A fiasco," Harris said. "Where is Dragan now?"

"Deceased. What choice did I have? He put everything at risk."

"And why do we care about Middleton?"

Vukasin took the picture from her. "This other man is Henryk Jedynak, a collector and expert in rare music documents. Jedynak is no longer with us either. You can ask Middleton why."

"I will gladly do so," Harris replied. "But

surely there is more to this than the death of music collector . . ."

Vukasin was tired, but it was the true she needed to know what the mission was. Now was a good time to tell her.

"Middleton was at St. Sophia with the peace keepers and he was among those given the task of cataloguing the musical manuscripts—the ones that remained at the church before we could remove them. Three years ago, Jedynak was asked to authenticate a few of the manuscripts Middleton left behind. When they were to be sold to a private collector, it was discovered that Jedynak replaced the manuscripts with fakes.

"The seller was Rugova," Vukasin added.

"And he expected a price sufficient to cover his costs of buying his freedom," Harris said.

"When I interrogated Jedynak, he admitted to his crime, but I could not persuade him to tell me where the original manuscripts were."

Harris smiled wryly. Vukasin knew only violence, and not the more subtle and sophisticated methods that were needed when interrogating true believers.

"He did tell me that Middleton was in possession of something he doesn't know he has, but would discover it soon enough."

"You squandered a valuable resource."

"I hardly need you to tell me what I have or haven't done."

But it was so. Jedynak had taken knowledge to the grave, and now his niece was gone too—stolen from under the noses of his men in Rome. What she knows remained a mystery.

Vukasin said, "I believe the key is somehow in a Chopin manuscript Jedynak gave to Middleton."

"Real or fake?" Harris asked.

Vukasin looked at her and raised an eyebrow. There was no reason to believe Jedynak could've known the real manuscript needed to be moved now. Vukasin had waited three years to seek its return.

Harris saw Vukasin bristle. "It was you who got to Rugova and his wife, wasn't it?" she asked, her voice rich with flattery.

Vukasin nodded. He was glad to tell her about how he'd accomplished the seemingly impossible.

"Colonel Rugova was desperate," he said. "Guards were bribed ahead of my visit, and I went in disguised as a lawyer from the Tribunal needing Rugova's signature on some documents. My fountain pen leaked, and the poisoned ink on the colonel's fingers did its job in seven or eight hours."

Vukasin smiled. "You know, the colonel was glad to see me. He was amused by my disguise, and very pleased when I told him we had a plan to get him to safety. He was unaware, of course, his wife had surrendered his journals—we had everything he was going to use for leverage. He even

106

named the men who paid him for the treasures—his benefactors. In the end, the great Colonel Rugova was a simple coward without loyalty or honor."

"I wish I could have been there."

Vukasin lit a small cigar and watched as a car pulled up. His two men exited and entered the hotel side by side.

"Now we'll see if Middleton is inside," he said.

"And if he's not . . . ?"

"His daughter," he replied. "Charlotte. Pregnant, by the way."

"Once I have Charlotte in the same room with him . . ." She smiled at the thought and rubbed her long delicate hands together vigorously. "Does he love anybody else?"

"A woman he worked with named Tesla. Leonora Tesla."

"If we had the Tesla woman, that might almost be as effective—if he still cares about her. But a pregnant daughter is preferable."

7

DAVID CORBETT

The car's interior reeked of almost archeological skank, old greasy food wrappers gumming the floor, malt liquor cans cluttering the wheel wells, ashtrays brimming with stale butts. The air-conditioner stuttered and coughed, exhaling a mildewy coolness, while the three bodies added an additional tang of gamey sweat—not just Middleton but Marcus and Traci, his would-be muggers. He'd learned their names from the non-stop badgering back and forth, relentless recriminations salted with snapshot details from their shattered biographies—their fumbling needs, their aching wants, their pitiless crank habits, promises to amend, curses in reply, testaments fired back and forth in a fierce vulgar slang that Middleton could barely decipher. Meanwhile, the car bumped and rattled north toward Baltimore, a lone headlight pointing the way along I-495's rain-wet asphalt. A brief summer storm had come and gone, turning the night air cottony thick and hot, against which the dying air-conditioner merely chattered. Middleton's sport jacket clung to his shoulders and arms like a second skin, and he wiped his face with his free hand, the other damply gripping the Beretta.

Finally, if only to ward off his nausea, he broke into the front-seat argument with, "Turn on the radio," nudging Marcus's shoulder with the pistol.

The youth turned just slightly. His cheek was mottled with small white sores. "Hey, me and Traci got things to discuss here."

Middleton lodged the tip of the pistol's barrel into Marcus's neck. "I said turn on the radio. I can't think."

"Don't jump the rail there, Mr. Gray." This was Traci, at the wheel, eyeing him over her shoulder. "You kidnap us, threaten us, we doin' all you ask. Be cool now. Don't play. Not with that gun."

They'd been calling him that since he'd climbed in the car: Mr. Gray. At first he'd thought it referred to his rumpled appearance, which was only worsening with the strain, the need for sleep. But he'd caught an edge of racial mockery in it too. Wasn't it Cab Calloway, in his Hepcat's Dictionary, who'd referred to white people as grays? But that was so very long ago, before these two were born. Christ, before even Middleton himself was born . . .

"I'm not playing," he said.

"All I mean—"

"Turn on the damn radio!"

Marcus's hand shot toward the dash and punched the On button. Middleton recoiled at the instant blast of menace, a lilting growl of bragging bullshit warring with a jackhammer bass track and droning synthesized mush, all inflicted at ear-splitting volume.

"Change the station."

"Whoa, mack, you got a serious pushy streak."

"Change the station. Now!"

Marcus huffed but obliged, fiddling through crackling sheets of white noise, punctuated by sudden twangy cries, garbled Bible-drunk voices . . .

Traci said, "You need to put a chill on, Mr. Gray. Break it back, let the little shit slide."

Suddenly, the reedy cry of woodwinds broke through. A soprano lilting through a familiar bar of haunting Sprechstimme. Middleton shot forward. "There! Stop!"

Marcus looked like he'd been told to swallow a toad. "This?"

"Tune it in. Get rid of the static."

"No, no. Taking us prisoner, that's wack enough. You can't torture us too."

"Tune it in!"

The piece was Pierrot Lunaire by Schoenberg, 21 songs scored for five musicians on eight instruments, plus voice, with the lyrics half-sung, half-spoken, the first twelve-tone masterpiece of the 20th century. Incomprehensible noise to most people, but not to Middleton, not to anyone who understood, who could hear in it the last throes of Romanticism, with echoes of not just Mahler and Strauss, but Bach.

"Maybe you're the one who should chill," Middleton said, easing back in his seat a little. "You think your generation invented rap or hip-hop? Spoken word with musical background goes back over four hundred years. It's called recitatif. Here, though, Schoenberg's notes are scored, but in speech we never stay on a single pitch, our voices glide on and off a tone. That's what the soprano's doing. It's left entirely up to her how she does it. Meanwhile, the instruments are conjuring up the landscape: there's moonlight, insanity, blood . . ."

Traci was leaning ever so slightly toward the speaker, intrigued now.

Eyeing the Beretta with a newfound skepticism, Marcus said, "You a professor?"

"Sshhh." It was Traci. The gaunt young coffee-skinned woman with glowing eyes and mussed Afro was rapt. "Act like you got some sense."

Sulking, Marcus flopped back against the door, moodily scratching his scabbed arm.

Finally, they were quiet; Middleton had his chance to think. But the eerie music, with its tale of the moon-obsessed clown and his Freudian nightmares, only enhanced his dread. Where was Charley, was she safe? Who tried to kill him at Dulles, what was the man after? And what was waiting for him at 122 Fremont Avenue, in the city of Baltimore?

The possible danger to Charley only amplified

the need to decipher the threat. His mind spun around and around like that, addled by the fatigue, his fear, thoughts careening against each other senselessly. Meanwhile:

> With a white speck of the bright moon
> On the shoulder of his black frock coat,
> Pierrot saunters off this languid evening
> To seek his fortune and look for adventure . . .

Nodding toward the radio, Marcus said, "Sounds like the same old screechy shit, over and over."

"Not if you understand German." Middleton rubbed his burning eyes. "And you're not listening to the accompaniment."

"It's edgy," Traci offered, striving for a compliment, though she'd clearly lost interest already.

Marcus sniffed. "Sounds like some kind of secret code, you ask me."

"Funny you should say that." Middleton stared out the grimy window at the blurring trees. "There were rumors during World War II that the Nazis were using twelve-tone music to send messages to sympathizers in the American cultural elite. There's no standard melody, people can't pick out a wrong note—"

"Sounds like nothing but wrong notes."

"Exactly. All the easier to hide a message in it. Who's going to know when the music is off?"

He flashed on the Chopin manuscript in his

briefcase, the one he'd thought the Polish authorities had wanted when they'd stopped him at the Krakow airport. His conviction it wasn't genuine lay exactly in several passages of oddly discordant cadences, unlike the meticulously melodic Chopin. What if it's a code, he wondered. What if it's not the manuscript or the other music they're after, but something far more valuable, something only to be found by decrypting the counterfeit folios?

Inspired suddenly, he reached down for his briefcase to check the manuscript—only to realize the briefcase wasn't there.

No please, he thought. Dear God. He mentally backtracked to the St. Regis, remembered placing his cell phone in his pocket at the restroom sink, then shambling out to the bar, checking his ravaged, hopelessly memorable reflection in the mirror before dropping the cell phone into his briefcase, snapping it shut. Had he then just wandered off without it? How dementedly absentminded. It was one more sign of how addled, scattered—moonstruck, like mad Pierrot—he'd become.

"Turn the car around."

Traci glowered over her shoulder. "Come again?"

"Turn the car around! We're going back to the hotel."

The two hapless thieves glanced back and forth. Marcus said, "Check out your eyes, mack."

Traci chimed in, "You beginning to scare me, Mr. Gray."

Middleton lifted the Beretta, placed the tip of the barrel against the back passenger-side window, and pulled the trigger. The thundering report in the small car, topped by the piercing hiss of shattered glass, deafened him again. Traci opened her mouth in a silent scream, hunching forward in terror as she fumbled to maintain hold of the steering wheel. Marcus clutched his head, staring at the gun with wide-eyed dread. The burnt sulfur smell of cordite, fanned by the sudden gust of black wet summer heat, finally masked the stench of the car's moldering interior.

Middleton reached forward, clutched Marcus's collar with his free hand while jabbing the pistol forward. As before at the airport, every sound came swathed in invisible muck, and yet from somewhere deep within his thrumming skull he heard the underwater roar of his own words, shouted at Traci: "I said turn the car around or I swear to God I'll kill him—I'll kill him, understand? Right here. I'll kill you too."

Struggling weakly in Middleton's grip, Marcus started to tremble uncontrollably. Reaching across the car, Traci tried to soothe him, the lilt of her gentling words finally beginning to register as, with a hateful glance over her shoulder, she merged right to make the coming exit.

Gradually, even the crackling radio, the abstract insistence of Pierrot Lunaire, returned. Middleton wondered: Who have I become?

Conrad the bartender held the manuscript, paging through it gingerly. It seemed very old—the paper faded and brittle, the notations handwritten, not printed like the ones he'd bought Jennifer before. She'd love this, he thought, feeling a surge of inner heat. Chopin. She'll throw her arms around his neck, press her cheek to his.

He lived to dote on his niece, buy her things— toys when she was younger, bits of modest clothing, sheet music now that she'd started piano lessons. A gifted girl, his sister's oldest, just turned nine. Growing a little awkward now that she was shooting up in height, leaving the baby fat behind, but still with that shimmering black hair, halfway down her back, the vaguely lost blue eyes, the porcelain skin. Black Irish, like her wretch of a father, wherever he might be. Prison. The grave. Back in Carrickfergus. Someone had to look after the girl, she needed a man in her life. And her uncle loved her. He loved her very much.

Her musical turn the past two years had proved a welcome change. He didn't have to just sit on the sofa and watch her gambol about on the floor in her school jumper and socks. He could sit there beside her now, turning the pages as she played the Schumann he'd bought her. Scenes from a

Childhood. Album for the Young. With the vanilla scent of her shampoo thick between them, her hands faltering in painful discords across the keys, he'd gently nudge closer, until their thighs touched, the rustle of her sleeve against his. That was enough, he'd remind himself. No more, not yet. Content yourself with this. But someday. Perhaps. If she wants to.

Such thoughts, such images, so terrible, so welcome, like the devil whispering in his ear: It's what you've always wanted. He lived for that, too.

He let the warmth subside from his face as he rolled up the manuscript and put it in the pocket of his sport jacket, draped on its peg on the storeroom wall. As he returned to the bar, two men entered from the hotel lobby, dressed in blue sport coats and gray slacks, one of them tall with an edgy fluid rhythm in his gait. The other was broad and muscular, with a bull-like neck, small dead eyes. The tall one offered an empty smile and slid a business card across the bar. It bore the seal of the FBI. Behind him, the hefty one remained expressionless.

There was no one else in the bar. It had been deathly slow all night.

The tall one, leaning forward to read the bartender's nametag, said, "Good evening, Conrad. A middle-aged man came in earlier, probably a little uneasy, rattled. He shot a peace officer out at the Dulles airport, then fled the scene. We have some indication the shooting may be terrorist-related. His cell phone placed him here just a short while back. It's very important we track his whereabouts. You recall him, yes?"

Conrad knew exactly the man they were talking about, but he couldn't convince himself just yet that admitting as much was wise. "The description you just gave," he said, "that could fit just about every guy who's been in here the past few hours. I mean, I'd like to help, but—"

The tall one wasn't listening. He'd spotted the briefcase behind the bar.

It belonged to the stranger from earlier, the one who looked like he'd wandered in from a car wreck. A cop-killer, they said. Apparently, a musical one. Conrad had found his briefcase while straightening the barstools, and he'd glanced inside, hoping to find some identification, only to discover the Chopin instead.

The tall one refreshed his vacant smile. "Would you mind handing that to me?" He nodded toward the briefcase and held out his hand. "I'd like to take a glance inside."

Conrad hesitated, yielding to an inchoate fear of being found out.

"Just to be clear, Conrad. National security's involved. We have broad powers. So." He wiggled his fingers. "If you would please."

Conrad collected the briefcase and handed it across the bar, figuring he had little choice. The tall one took it greedily and immediately opened it up, searching the contents brusquely. His partner just stood there, a little ways behind, his huge arms folded across his massive chest.

"It's not here," the tall one said finally. He looked over his shoulder at his partner, then back toward Conrad. The empty smile was now pitiless. "Something's missing. But you know that already—don't you, Conrad?"

Conrad felt the floor sway beneath him, his viscera coiled. An inner voice said, They're going to find out your dirty little secret. Before he could think through the consequences, he heard himself say, "I don't know what you mean," his voice faltering. He pictured Jennifer sitting sad-eyed and prim on her shiny black piano bench, waiting for her only uncle, smelling of breath mints and aftershave, to settle in beside her.

"The sheet music, Conrad. It's supposed to be inside. It's not. Fetch it for us now. Before I lose my temper."

It was only then that Conrad realized what it was that bothered him about the man's voice. The accent. Canadian, he thought. Can Canadians join the FBI?

"Look, I'm not trying to be difficult, but I honestly don't know what you're talking about."

The tall one glanced past the bartender to the storeroom door; they'd seen him closing it behind him as they'd entered from the lobby. The agent nodded for his muscular partner to have a look.

"You can't go back there." Conrad felt a trickle of sweat feathering down his back.

"And why is that?"

"It's hotel property."

The tall man grinned. "And?"

The hefty one was behind the bar now. He gave Conrad a snide pat on the cheek, then opened the storeroom door.

His partner said, "It's in your best interests to offer full cooperation. I'm a little disappointed I have to explain that."

"You get out first."

Middleton waved Marcus onto the sidewalk with the Beretta. Opening his own door, he sent one last shower of broken glass tumbling, the spiny fragments toppling down his sleeve. Closing the door behind him, he told Traci through the jagged maw where the window had been, "Wait here. There's something I left behind. We'll only be a minute."

The young woman said nothing, just sat there gripping the wheel, seething.

Middleton plunged the pistol into his sport-coat pocket, taking Marcus's elbow and gripping it tight. "Come on. We'll make this quick."

They were halfway between the street and the hotel's revolving door when the car peeled out behind them. Both of them turned, watching Traci flee, Middleton feeling his jaw drop. The car reached the corner in one long burst of speed, then a squeal of brakes, a swerving turn. Gone.

Before Middleton could gather his wits, the youth shook off his grip and swept a cracking left across Middleton's jaw, then darted off, running as fast as his stick-thin legs could carry him. Reeling back on his heels, Middleton gathered his balance but then just stared, rubbing his stubbled chin as the scrawny boy vanished down the wet street.

An hour's gone by, Middleton thought, since I last stood here, this very spot. Nothing's changed. Except, perhaps, everything.

He entered the lobby wiping his face with his handkerchief, hoping he didn't look as raw and untethered as he felt. The desk clerk, recognizing him from earlier, smiled blankly. A well-dressed woman with a slim valise, possibly a call girl, waited at the elevator.

Finding his way to the small dark bar, Middleton crossed the threshold, then stopped. The bartender was wrestling with a man much bigger than he was, while another, taller man looked on. The two strangers were dressed almost identically: blue blazers and gray slacks, Oxford button-downs and forgettable ties, none of which matched their demeanor. The tall one looked on with a cold curiosity; sadism curdled his smile. He held Middleton's briefcase in his hand while examining a cell phone that Middleton quickly recognized as his. Meanwhile, the other one, who looked much stronger, had the bartender in a headlock, punching him brutally with his free hand. The bartender's arm was outstretched, the Chopin folio clutched tight in his fist.

As Middleton registered all this, the one with the briefcase turned toward him. You have no time, Middleton realized, as a scowl of recognition crossed the other man's face. Tugging the Beretta from his pocket, Middleton charged forward as the man dropped the cell phone and plunged his hand inside his sport coat. Middleton aimed and placed two quick shots into the fleshy center of the tall man's face, trusting the bullets would pierce the cartilage around the nose and lodge deep inside the brain.

The man tottered, his head jerking but his ugly expression strangely unchanged. Then he buckled and dropped.

Stunned by the gunshots, the thick man shoved the bartender aside and crouched, reaching for his own weapon. Middleton swung around, took a quick step forward, aimed and fired two more shots, close range, the soft center of the face again. The man wavered, visage threaded with blood, before dropping to one knee, grabbing at the edge of the bar, then sliding down in fitful spasms.

The bartender recoiled, horrified. Middleton heard steps coming from the lobby, the gasps of unseen onlookers, as he reached out his hand.

"Give that to me." He gestured for the manuscript. When the bartender merely stared, Middleton turned the gun toward him. "I don't have time."

The bartender hesitated, then dropped the mangled folio onto the bar, his face half terror, half desolation. Middleton snatched his briefcase from the floor, stuffed his cell phone then the manuscript inside, then headed toward the scattering crowd in the lobby, the Beretta still in his hand.

The well-dressed woman who'd been near the elevators earlier slipped up behind, tucked her hand inside his arm and clutched his damp sleeve. She guided him across the lobby. "Don't stop, Harry," she whispered. "Not if you want to see Charlotte."

8

JOHN GILSTRAP

Felicia Kaminski had always loved the idea of airports. As a child in a family that never went anywhere, she used to envy the friends who would take their holidays in places that were far enough away to be flown to. Trains were a thrill in their own right, but only at airports did you find people who are going far enough away to actually change their lives. Having dreamed of the moment for so long, she was finally about to climb on her very first airplane—to fly to the United States. In first class, no less.

Fiumicino International Airport teemed with travelers mingling in their common mission to check in and navigate their way to their departure gates. Felicia Kaminski—no, Joanna Phelps; she might have to remember that—found herself distracted by one family in particular as a mother and father did their best to herd six children toward the security lines. It looked a lot like pushing water up hill. She found herself smiling.

Then she forced herself to concentrate. After this morning's events, she needed to be vigilant. Clearly, she was a target and if another attacker wanted to hurt her, she would most certainly be hurt. It helped that every 10th person in the airport was a carabinieri with a machine gun slung over his shoulder. It seemed to her like a very bad place to attempt murder.

The afternoon's events were unfolding exactly as Faust had predicted. Freshly cleaned and redressed, he'd led her downstairs through the lobby of the hotel, where two Mercedes sedans stood waiting with their engines running. He ushered her to the first vehicle while he climbed into the back seat of the other. They'd pulled away from the curb together, but then split into different directions, her car going right while his went left, and she hadn't seen any sign of him since.

"I understand that you haven't traveled much," her driver said in passable Polish. She couldn't quite place the accent. "Do you know how the check-in process works?"

Kaminski hated the patronizing tone, but had to confess her ignorance. The driver—Peter, if he'd told her the truth—took her through the process step by step, from check-in at the ticket counter, to the passage through security, and on to the boarding process itself. The only real surprise came from the requirement to take her shoes off to go through the metal detectors. She was well aware of the detectors themselves, of course, but it just hadn't occurred to her that she would have to strip off articles of clothing.

"Are you going to walk through the process with me?" she'd asked when Peter had finished.

"No, Miss Phelps, I'm afraid that will not be possible. Security at the airport is very tight these days. I must stay with the car and drive away as soon as I drop you off. You will be on your own."

"Where is Faust?"

Peter's eyes found hers in the rearview mirror. For a long moment, he said nothing. "He will be where he needs to be at the correct time. What is most important is that you remember to show no sign of recognition if you see him again. Let him make that move."

"I remember," she said. I'm in no hurry to know him anyway.

Having arrived at the airport with nearly three hours to spare, Felicia moved quickly to get through the check-in process at the ticket counter, but then took her time heading for security. Befitting her first-class status, Faust had given her 300 U.S. dollars to fill her wallet, and she decided to put some of the windfall to good use at an airport coffee shop. She found a table at the edge of the concourse, one that offered a broad view of the security lines. It was a sea of people, shoulder to shoulder in a human corral.

On the far side of the crowd, she could see the first-class security area, where the crowds were much thinner and better organized, and that was where she concentrated her attention. It was there that she predicted that things were about to get exciting.

It took long enough that she had to order a second espresso—surrendering herself to the inevitability of being wide-eyed all night—but after 45 minutes, she saw what she'd been waiting for. Faust finally entered the line. In his business attire, he looked completely at home among the other wealthy travelers.

From 15 meters away, she watched as the man who'd saved her life shrugged out of his suit jacket and stepped out of his shoes. He placed his brief-case on the belt for the x-ray machine, then stepped through the narrow archway of the metal detector.

Kaminski's heart hammered against her ribs as she began to wonder if something had gone wrong. There should be a reaction by now. There should—

Suddenly, an alarm erupted and a red light strobed urgently over the security checkpoint. It was the kind of noise and light that guaranteed attention and made people instinctively want to run away. All except for the carabinieri, that is, who swarmed from all over the concourse to respond to the threat.

Biting the inside of her cheek to stifle any sign of the satisfied smile that might draw attention to her, Kaminski pushed away from the table and started walking toward the taxi stands at the front of the airport. Before that, she needed to find a cambio, where she could convert her windfall of U.S. dollars into more readily spent euros. She knew she had time—Faust would be busy with the cara-binieri for at least a couple of hours, she imag-ined—and she hoped that even a short delay would provide enough time for her to do what she needed to do and then disappear.

Meanwhile, the officials at the airport would be turning Faust's luggage inside out as they looked for the pistol that showed up so clearly in the x-ray. Ultimately, probably in fairly short order, they'd find the source of their alarm.

She wondered if any of them would even smile when they realized that they'd mobilized dozens of policia because a businessman had covered a water pistol with a foil wrapper and stuffed it in one of the file pockets of his brief case.

Felicia Kaminski left the airport with none of her new clothes—none but what she wore, that is. Her fancy new suitcase was somewhere in the bowels of the airport, already checked and on its way to the aircraft that would dead-head it to New York. She kept the money too, but beyond that, she car-ried only those items that were rightfully hers—her backpack and her violin.

She had the taxi drop her at the foot of Via dei Polacchi, and she added a generous tip to the fare. What was the point of a windfall if it couldn't be shared with others? The driver thanked her effu-sively and offered three times to wait for her while she ran whatever errand she was on, but after she'd steadfastly refused, he finally understood that her insistent "no" meant just that, and he drove on.

She waited until the taxi was out of sight around the corner before she started walking up the hill. She'd never actually visited the shop she was looking for—La Musica—but she'd sipped coffee with Abe Nowakowski, the proprietor, several times since she'd arrived in Rome. Signor Abe and her uncle had shared a childhood, it turned out, living only a few houses away from each other in the old country. Uncle Henryk had asked his friend to look in on her from time to time. During their last meeting, at a cafe near the Pantheon, only a few dozen meters from the spot where she had first encountered the man who called himself Faust, Abe's demeanor had been different than it had been before. His easy humor seemed clouded by something dark.

During one of her visits, she asked, "Are you feeling all right?"

He'd smiled, but it wasn't convincing. "I am just getting old, that is all," he said. He paused a moment before adding, "I am concerned for you, Felicia."

So that was it. "I enjoy my life, Signor Abe. I understand that you worry about me, but as I've told you before—"

He cut her off with a dismissive flick of his hand. "I know what you have to say, so let's pretend that you have already said it and move on. I want you to promise me something."

She cocked her head, waiting. When dealing with her uncle's generation, it never paid to make a promise before all terms had been revealed.

"If anything happens to you, if ever you are in any trouble, I want you to come to me."

Looking back on the conversation now, she wondered if Signor Abe hadn't known something. Even at the time, she'd felt her pulse quicken with his sense of urgent mystery.

He'd read her expression exactly, and hurried to soothe her. "I don't mean to frighten you," he'd said. "As I get older I sometimes worry about things that perhaps I shouldn't. But if there ever comes a time when you feel as if you are in danger—or even if there comes a time when you merely feel lonely or hungry for some of my fettuccini—I want you to promise that you will come by the shop. I worry that I am not showing you the hospitality that I should. I don't want to disappoint my dear friend Henryk."

That conversation had taken place only two weeks ago. Now, as she walked purposefully up the hill, she forced her mind to think of music. If she could bridge the synapses of her brain with triplettes and chromatic scales, maybe there would be no room left for her fear. No room left for the looming grief that awaited her when she finally confronted the fact of her uncle's death.

She walked faster. The increased tempo brought to her imagination the sound of

American bluegrass music—fiddle music instead of the violin—a music form that she'd never taken seriously until she'd listened to a CD that featured Yo Yo Ma bringing sounds out of his cello that she had never heard before. She heard alternating strains of joy and melancholy. She'd tried to recreate the sounds in her own violin, but could never quite discover them. It was as if those particular strands of musical DNA could not be found in an instrument played by a Polish girl whose childhood was steeped in classical training.

Kaminski saw the sign for La Musica from a block away, and instantly wished that the walk could have been longer. With a few more steps, perhaps she could have found the emotional strength she craved, the strength she needed before breaking terrible news to such a nice man. But it was not to be. She had arrived, and she could think of no reason not to enter the shop.

Passing across the threshold was like stepping backward a hundred years. Narrow, dark and deep, the shop reminded her of a cave; where there would be bats, dozens of violins and violas and cellos hung instead from the ceiling, each of them glimmering as if they'd been freshly dusted. Double basses lined the left-hand wall, and along the right, countless pages of sheet music peeked out from above their wooden racks. At the very back of the store . . .

Actually, she couldn't see the back of the store through the shadows that cloaked it.

"Felicia?"

The voice came from behind her—from the cash register she had not seen, hidden away as it was around the corner at the very front of the store. She instantly recognized the heavily accented voice as that of Signor Abe, but she jumped anyway as she whirled to look at him.

"Felicia, what's wrong?" Even as he spoke, he was on his way around to the front of the tiny counter, moving as quickly as his arthritic hips would allow him. "What has happened?"

The flood of emotion hit out of nowhere, all at once. "Uncle Henryk is dead," she managed to say, but her next words were lost in her sobs.

Abe Nowakowski locked the door to his shop at mid-day, something he'd never done before, and helped his beautiful young friend up the back steps to his flat on the second floor. There he fixed her some tea and listened to her story.

Kaminski hated herself for losing control of her emotions this way, but there were times in the next hour when she feared that her tears would never stop. They did, of course, eventually, but she sensed that Signor Abe would have sat with her for as long as he needed to.

"These things take time," he said. He was a little man, a round man, with leathery skin and thick white hair that could never be tamed by a comb. When he spoke softly like this, his normally strong voice grew raspy. "I lost my Maria six years ago now, and while sometimes it feels as though the hole in my heart has healed, there are days when the pain is as raw as the day she died. I've come to think of the pain as proof that I loved her as much as I told her I did."

The tea was awful, overly strong and overly sweet. "Did you know this might happen to my uncle, Signor Abe?" she asked.

The question seemed to startle the old man.

"The other day, when we met for coffee, you asked me to make a promise. I made it, and here I am. But I was wondering . . ."

She let her voice trail as Signor Abe let his gaze fall to his lap. The body language answered her question; now she hoped that he wouldn't dishonor her uncle's memory with a transparent lie to protect her feelings.

"I had an inkling, yes," he said. "Your uncle called me shortly before you and I met. He seemed . . . agitated. He spoke hurriedly, as if he were trying to get his message out before he could be interrupted. Or perhaps before he could change his mind." Nowakowski took a deep breath and let it go slowly. When he resumed speaking, his rasp had deepened. "He told me that he would be sending me a package for safe keeping. He said that it would be too dangerous for him to have the package with him and that by sending it to me it would truly be safe."

"Did the package come?"

He ignored the interruption. "I of course agreed, but then he called the very next day. This time, he was clearly frightened. He said that he hadn't thought things through very clearly before he mailed it and he was terrified that people might think that he had sent it to you instead. It's what people would naturally think of anything he sent to Rome. He asked me to check in with you more frequently and to try and find out if you had been in any danger. He wanted me to do this without alarming you, of course."

"What kind of danger?"

The old man rose from the table to return to the stove. "Before today, I wouldn't have been able to tell you. I think now we know. More tea, Felicia?"

She recoiled from the thought and tried to cover the reaction with, "I've been drinking coffee all day. I don't need my hands to shake more than they already do."

Nowakowski gave a knowing smile and limped back to the table. "Yes, I've been told that I make it a bit too strong. One of the hazards of not having very many guests, I suppose."

"About the package," she pressed. "Did you ever receive it?"

"I did." He spoke the words as if his explanation was complete.

"What was it?"

Signor Abe's gaze dropped again. Kaminski realized that this was his habit when he was embarrassed. "Dear Henryk asked me specifically not to open the package when it arrived. He told me that it would arrive double-wrapped, and that if anything ever happened to him, I was to open only the outer wrapping and then contact the name I found on the card taped to the inner wrapping."

"But you opened it anyway," she said, connecting the dots.

"Loneliness breeds weakness and curiosity," he replied sadly. "And I'm afraid that I have been particularly lonely."

"So what was in it?" She found the old man's embarrassment charming, but she'd have ripped it open in a second if she'd have been in his place. No reason for shame there.

He thought for a moment, and then rose again from his chair. He disappeared into what must have been the bedroom, and then returned less than a minute later with a thick, mangled envelope. "I tried to re-wrap it," he confessed, "but I'm afraid I made something of a mess."

The envelope was a large one, more suitable to construction blueprints than a letter. He handled the package gently, with reverence, almost, as he placed it onto the table between them. When Felicia reached toward it, he shooed her hands away.

"Please," he said curtly. "Allow me to do this."

She folded her hands on her lap.

The old man wiped his hands aggressively with a napkin, and then carefully slid the contents into the daylight.

Kaminski leaned closer. She saw a stack of papers. Her first impression was that it was very old—yellow with the kinds of marks that could only be made with an old style ink pen. As more of the contents were revealed, she squinted and leaned even closer. "It's a musical score," she said, recognizing the rows of staves.

Nowakowski allowed himself a conspiratorial smile. "Much more than that," he said. He gently placed it on top of the envelope and turned it so that she could better read his treasure.

My God. Could it be what she thought? There was no mistaking the long runs of sixteenth notes and the other musical notations, but as exotic as they looked written by hand, her eyes were drawn to the written signature at the top. In her circles, there was no more famous a signature.

"Mozart?" she gasped.

"An original," he beamed. "Or at least I think it is."

She didn't know what to say. "It must be worth a fortune."

"Three fortunes," he corrected. "Priceless, I would think. It's clearly a piano concerto, but I've searched the Koechel Catalogue and this isn't there. I think this is an undiscovered work."

She recognized the Koechel Catalogue as the internationally recognized indexer of Mozart's myriad compositions. If Signor Abe was right, then there truly was no way to estimate the value of the manuscript. "This is fabulous," she said. "But I don't understand why it frightened Uncle Henryk. This could have answered all of his wildest dreams. Honestly, this is the kind of discovery that he would have given anything to make. Why would he keep it a secret? Why would he send it away?"

"All very good questions," Nowakowski agreed. "But I have an even bigger one."

She waited for it while the old man slid the inner envelope out from under the manuscript. She saw a name, but there was no address.

He said, "Who is this Harold Middleton and how are we supposed to find him?"

9

JOSEPH FINDER

The moment her Nextel phone chirped, Special Agent M. T. Connolly had a bad feeling.

She'd just gotten into the elevator at the brand-new building that housed the FBI's Northern Virginia Resident Agency, on her way back to her office. It was a cubicle, actually, not an office, but she could always dream.

Glancing at the caller ID, she immediately recognized the area code and exchange prefix: the call came from the Hoover building—FBI headquarters in D.C. Not good. Only bad news came from the Hoover building, she'd learned. She stepped out of the elevator and back onto the gleaming terrazzo floor of the lobby.

"Connolly," she said.

A man's voice, reedy and overly precise: "This is Emmett Kalmbach."

He didn't actually have to identify himself; she'd have recognized the prissy enunciation anywhere. Kalmbach was the FBI's Assistant Director who oversaw the hundreds of agents in D.C. and Virginia who worked out of the Washington Field Office as well as her satellite office in Manassas, Virginia. She'd met Kalmbach a few times, enough to recognize his type: the worst kind of kiss-up, kick-down bureaucratic infighter. A paper-pushing rattlesnake.

Kalmbach had no reason to call her directly. At least, no good reason. And why was he calling from the FBI's national headquarters, instead of from his office on Fourth Street?

"Yes, sir," she said. She sounded blasé, but she felt her stomach clench. She watched the brushed-steel elevator doors glide shut in front of her. The two halves of a giant fingerprint, etched on the elevator doors, came together. The fingerprint had been some government committee's idea of art, which was precisely what it looked like: art by government committee.

"Agent Connolly, who is Jozef Padlo?"

Ah ha. "He's an inspector with the Polish National Police and he's working a triple homicide in Warsaw that—"

"Agent—Marion, if I may—"

"M. T., sir."

But he went on smoothly, ignoring her: "—Our legat in Warsaw just emailed me a letter rogatory from the Polish Ministry of Justice, requesting that we grant immediate entry into the U.S. to this . . . Jozef Padlo. He says you personally guaranteed him clearance. Our legat is understandably ticked off."

So this was what he was calling about. She hadn't gone through channels, so some junior FBI paper-pusher, who'd picked the short straw and had ended up assigned to the American Embassy Bureau in Warsaw, had gotten bent out of shape.

"Obviously there was some translation problem," she said. "I didn't guarantee anything to Inspector Padlo. He's provided invaluable assistance to us in a case at Dulles involving the murder of one, possibly two, cops. Since it seems to be connected to his triple homicide, he—"

"It 'seems to be connected,'" Kalmbach interrupted. "What's that supposed to mean?"

Trying to conceal her annoyance, she explained as crisply as she could. "Padlo was able to ID the shooter at Dulles as a Serb national and a war criminal who—"

"Excuse me, Agent Connolly. He ID'd the shooter based on what?"

"Surveillance video taken at Dulles."

"Ah. So Inspector Padlo viewed the video, then?"

She faltered. "No. I did. But Padlo made a positive ID based on my verbal description to him."

"Your . . . verbal description," Kalmbach echoed softly. Condescension dripped from every word.

"In fact—" she began, but Kalmbach cut her off.

"Do you understand how complex and involved the process is by which a foreign law enforcement official is granted entry into the United States? It involves weeks of legal findings and sworn affidavits by the DOJ's Criminal Division, the Office of International Affairs. It's a cumbersome and extremely sensitive legal affair and not one to be taken lightly. For one thing, there must be absolutely incontrovertible evidence of dual criminality."

Oh, for God's sake, she thought. The guy lived and breathed paperwork. It was a wonder he hadn't already died of white lung. "Sir, if Padlo's right then, those three homicides in Warsaw are tied to these police shootings at Dulles Airport and we've got a clear-cut case of dual criminality."

"A case built on a verbal description over the telephone, Agent Connolly? I hardly think that constitutes a finding of dual criminality. This is an awfully slender reed. I'm afraid we're not going to be able to grant a visa to Inspector Padlo."

Yeah, she thought. If Jozef wanted to get into the country quick and easy, no questions asked, he should just join Al Qaeda and enroll in flight school. We'd let him in without a second look.

But she said, "So you're saying that if we had a clear-cut ID of the shooter—connecting the Warsaw homicides to the Dulles ones—you'd have no problem letting Padlo in?"

"We don't have that, do we?" Kalmbach said acidly.

"No, sir," she said. "Not yet."

"Thank you, Agent . . . Marion."

"M. T.," she said.

But he'd hung up.

• • •

She'd been M. T. since the age of thirteen.

She'd always hated her given name, "Marion." Her father had also been Marion; but then, as he was always proud to point out, that was John Wayne's real name. In Gulfport, Mississippi, where Dad had been a part-time deputy in the Harrison County Sheriff's Department, the Duke was up there with Jesus Christ. Bigger, to some folks.

But to her, "Marion" was either a librarian or a housewife in a TV sitcom, and neither fit her self-image. She was a tomboy and proud of it. As tough as any boy, she had even beat up the seventh-grade class bully for daring to call her adored younger brother Wayne a "sissy."

So she insisted on being called by her initials, which to her ears sounded tough and no-nonsense and the exact opposite of girly-girl. Maybe even a little enigmatic.

Over the years, she'd learned about makeup, and she'd developed a pretty damned nice figure, and she worked out every morning at five for at least an hour. When she wanted to look hot, she could. And she knew that when she put on that slinky red jersey halter dress from Banana Republic she always drew appreciative glances from men.

At work, though, she downplayed her femininity as much as possible. The FBI was still a boys' club, and she was convinced that the guys took you a lot more seriously if you didn't arouse their libidos.

Like the guy who sat across from her right now. His name was Bruce Ardsley, and he was a forensic video analyst with the Bureau's Forensic Audio, Video, and Image Analysis Unit. The main FBI lab was in D.C., in the Hoover building, but they'd recently installed an outpost here because of all the demand on the Bureau since 9/11.

Ardsley wore thick aviator-frame glasses and had greasy hair and long bushy sideburns that might have been modish in the Swinging '70s, and he was notorious for trying to hit on all the female agents and administrative assistants. But he'd given up on her long ago. Now they got along fine.

His office, in the basement of the new resident agency building, was no bigger than a closet, jammed with steel shelves heaped with video monitors and digital editing decks and CPUs. Taped to one wall was a mangled poster of a man running up stadium steps. Above his blurred figure was the word PERSISTENCE. At his feet it said, "There is no GIANT step that does it. It's a lot of LITTLE steps."

She handed Ardsley two disks. "The one marked Dulles is from Dulles Airport," Connolly said.

"Clever."

She smiled. "The other has the photos from Warsaw." As he promised, Padlo had emailed her photos of Agim Rugova's henchmen. One of them was Dragan Stefanovic, the man Padlo thought might be the Dulles shooter who'd tried to kill Harold Middleton. Stefanovic had served under Agim Rugova, which made him a war criminal at the very least. After the war, Padlo said, he'd become a mercenary and had gone into hiding.

"High-def, I hope."

"I doubt it," she replied.

"Well, all I can do is my best," Ardsley said. "At least one thing in our favor is the new networked digital-video surveillance system at Dulles. The airports authority dumped a boatload of money on this a couple years ago. Bought a bunch of high-priced Nextiva S2600e wide-dynamic range IP cameras with on-board analytical software-based solutions."

"Translation, please," said Connolly.

"Meaning the facial-recognition software is still crap and the images are still fuzzy, but now we can all feel good about how much money we're throwing at the terrorists."

"And that's in our favor . . . how exactly?" she asked.

He pointed to the steel shelves lined with video monitors. "Once the Bureau realized how crappy the facial-recognition system is, they were forced to sink more money into toys for boys like me to play with. Remember the Super Bowl?"

She groaned. The FBI had put in an extensive surveillance system at the Super Bowl in Tampa in

2001 in order to scan the faces of everyone passing through the turnstiles and match them against the images of known terrorists. The ACLU pitched a fit—this was before 9/11, when people listened to the ACLU—but the whole scheme was a resounding flop anyway. The Bureau had rounded up a couple of scalpers and that was it. "You're telling me the technology's no better now?"

"Oh, it's better," Ardsley said. "Well, a little better."

Her phone chirped, and she excused herself and stepped out into the hallway.

"Connolly."

"Hey, M. T., it's Tanya Jackson in Technical Services."

"That was fast," she said. "You got something?"

She'd called the FBI's Technical Services unit and asked them to run a locater on Middleton's cell phone to find out where he was at that very instant. Most cell phones these days, she knew, contained GPS chips that enabled you to pinpoint its location to within a hundred meters, as long as it was turned on and transmitting a signal.

"Well, not exactly," Jackson said. "There's sort of a procedural problem."

"Procedural? . . ."

"Look, M. T.," Jackson said apologetically, "you know we're no longer allowed to track cell phone users without a court order."

"Oh, is that right?" Connolly said innocently. Of

course, she knew all about the recent rulings. Now you had to get a court order to compel a wireless carrier to reveal the location of one of their cell phones. And to get a court order, you had to demonstrate that a crime was in progress or had occurred.

But Jackson had done her favors before. She'd located cell phones for Connolly without the necessary paperwork. Why did she all of a sudden care about the legal niceties?

"Tanya," she said, "what's going on?"

There was silence on the other end of the line.

"You're getting heat on this, aren't you?" Connolly said.

Another beat of silence, and then Jackson said, "Five minutes after you called me, I heard from someone pretty high up in the Bureau. He reminded me that it was a felony for me to locate a cell phone without a court order. I could go to jail."

"I'm sorry I put you in that position," Connolly said.

"I just wanted you to understand."

"Tanya," Connolly said. "Was it Emmett Kalmbach, by any chance?"

"I—I can't answer that," Jackson said.

But she didn't have to.

"You're in luck," Bruce Ardsley said. He was beaming.

"Dragan Stefanovic is the shooter?"

He nodded.

145

"How certain can you be?"

"Ninety-seven percent probability of true verification."

"Bruce, that's fantastic." Take that, Kalmbach, she thought.

"The probability on the other one's lower, though."

"The other one?"

"Maybe seventy-eight percent probability."

"Which other one are you talking about?"

Ardsley swiveled around in his chair, tapped at a keyboard, and a large photographic image came up on the flat-screen monitor mounted on the wall in front of her. It was a close-up of a dark-haired man in his 40s wearing a dark, expensive-looking business suit. He had flat, Slavic facial features.

"Where was this taken?"

"A surveillance camera outside a men's room in Concourse D at Dulles."

"Who is it?" she said.

"Nigel Sedgwick."

"Who?"

Ardsley struck another key, and a second photo popped onto the screen next to the first.

"A British businessman. From Bromsgrove, in Worcestershire. That's England. Or so his passport said. Here in D.C. on a buying trip for his hot-tub business."

"Looks like it was taken at passport control," she said.

Ardsley turned around, shrugged modestly, smiled. "Right."

"How'd you get it?"

"I hacked into Homeland Security. Well, not hacked, really. Just used a backdoor into Customs and Border Protection's database."

"So who is this guy really?"

A third image appeared on the screen next to the other two. She immediately recognized the photo as one of the mug shots of Agim Rugova's men that Padlo had emailed her.

"Vukasin," she said.

"He entered the country last night on a British Airways flight from Paris. Using a British passport."

Connolly nodded. "I guess Homeland Security doesn't have facial-recognition software, huh? Or they'd have stopped him."

"Oh, they have the software, believe me," he said. "Plus, this guy Vukasin is on one of their watch lists."

"Maybe their software isn't as good as ours."

"Or maybe someone knew who he was and let him in anyway."

"That doesn't make any sense," she said.

"A lot of what Homeland Security does makes no sense," Ardsley said.

"What are you saying—you think he was flagged as a bad guy but let through anyway?"

"Yes," Ardsley said. "That's what I think. But I'm only a video tech, so what do I know?"

"Jesus," she breathed.

"So let me ask you something," he said.

She turned away from the flat-screen. "Go ahead."

"You ever free for a drink?"

"You don't give up, do you?" Connolly said.

He pointed at the ripped motivational poster on the wall. "Persistence," he said with a sheepish smile.

As Connolly approached her cubicle, she saw from a distance that a man was sitting in her chair. Another man was standing next to him.

The man in the chair was Emmett Kalmbach. The man standing beside him was tall and wiry, with horn-rimmed glasses and a receding hairline. She had no idea who he was.

Then the standing man noticed her, muttered something, and Kalmbach turned slowly around.

"Agent Connolly," Kalmbach said, getting to his feet. "Allow me to introduce Richard Chambers from DHS."

She shook hands with the man in the horn-rimmed glasses. His handshake was cold and limp.

"Dick Chambers," the man said. He didn't smile.

"M. T. Connolly."

"Dick is a Regional Director of Homeland Security," Kalmbach said.

"A pleasure to meet you." Connolly kept her tone and face neutral, as if she'd never heard of him. But in fact she had. His background was almost clichéd diplomatic track: Yale, OCS, and then State Department. He'd been posted to some of the worst hotspots in the world. After September 11, he'd gone to Homeland Security, resolved that no terrorist would ever show his face in the Mid-Atlantic region of the country. Chambers wasn't popular among the feds—an abrasive façade over an ego that wouldn't quit—but he was a man who took on fires that nobody else wanted to go near. And, without any hesitation to risk his own hide, he got them extinguished. That he was involved made her uneasy. Real uneasy. "Now will someone explain to me what's going on?" she asked.

"We can talk in the conference room," Kalmbach said.

"Agent Connolly," the man from Homeland Security said, "we seem to have a communications problem that I hope we can all work out in person." He'd taken a seat at the head of the mahogany conference table, wordlessly indicating his place in the hierarchy.

"What sort of 'communication problem'?" she asked.

"Agent Connolly," Kalmbach said, "what happened at Dulles Airport falls cleanly within the jurisdiction of the Virginia police. I thought I made it clear that the situation there is of no concern to the Bureau."

That wasn't what he'd said, of course. He seemed to be performing for the man from DHS. But she knew better than to argue with Emmett Kalmbach over what he had or had not told her.

"Actually," Connolly said, holding up the CD that Bruce Ardsley had made for her, "I think it's very much of concern to the Bureau. Our own facial-recognition software has identified two Serbian war criminals who've entered the country illegally, one of them using a false British passport under the name—"

"Why are you trying to locate Harold Middleton?" Chambers interrupted, taking the disk from her hand.

"Because he's a material witness," Connolly said. "In an international case that involves a triple homicide in Warsaw, and another one, or possibly by now two—"

"Was I not absolutely clear?" Kalmbach said, his face flushing, but the DHS man put a hand on Kalmbach's sleeve, apparently to silence him.

"Agent Connolly," Chambers said softly, "Harold Middleton's file is blue-striped."

She looked at him, then nodded. A blue stripe indicated that a file was sealed for national-security reasons. Part of Middleton's military record had been designated as codeword-classified. That meant a level above even top secret.

"Why?" she asked finally.

Kalmbach scowled and said nothing. The man from Homeland replied, "How do I put this in a language you'll understand? This is above your pay grade, Agent Connolly."

"Meaning I'm off the case?" she blurted out.

"No, Agent Connolly," Chambers said. "Meaning that there is no case."

10

JIM FUSILLI

Leonora Tesla stepped out of the yellow taxi on the busy northwest corner of Sixth Avenue and 35th Street, and hustled into Macy's. She emerged with her hair trimmed short and punked, wearing a black button-down blouse with the collar curled high, black slacks and black flats— in many ways, the opposite of what she wore 24 hours earlier when she killed Günter Schmidt. A new black-leather shoulder bag, tucked tight under her arm, held a change of underwear and what remained from the moment she steered Schmidt's body toward the ravaging hyenas down in the wadi: her sunglasses, cash, credit cards and passport, her portfolio and her most valued possession, her fully loaded iPod, a gift from Harold Middleton.

She called the Human Rights Observer from a payphone in Herald Square. An intern answered and told her Val Brocco hadn't come in. A flu, she reported; his message said he intended to spend a second day in bed. Tesla decided against giving her name and demanding his latest cell number, consoling herself with the thought that Brocco's bordering-on-obsessive sense of precaution might serve him well. It'd better: To find Middleton, they'd tried to kill her, sending an agent to Namibia for the task. No doubt they already had at least one agent in metro D.C., where Middleton and Brocco were based.

Next, from the lobby of Madison Square Garden, she tried Jean-Marc Lespasse in Parkwood, North Carolina. Mr. Lespasse, she was told, was no longer with TDD—Technologie de Demain, the company he founded. And, no, the receptionist added tersely, there's no forwarding information. Sure enough, the last cell number Tesla had for Lespasse was no longer active.

Downstairs into Penn Station, Tesla paid cash for a one-way ticket on the Acela Express to Washington's Union Station, though she planned to get off in Delaware. Checking the overhead departure board, she saw she had enough time to run to the newsstand for a pre-paid cell phone and an array of domestic and international newspapers for the two-hour train ride to Wilmington.

As she gathered her change, she looked up. There, on a TV above a rack of batteries and disposable cameras, was a grainy video of a gun battle at Dulles Airport. "Two Cops Killed," the zipper reported.

"Harold," she said, the word escaping before she realized it had.

She stared at the soundless newscast. The zipper under the video now told her the gunman hadn't yet been found.

For some reason, she took it as verification that he was still alive.

She wondered if the same could be said of Lespasse and, maybe, Brocco.

Twelve hours earlier, Harold Middleton left the St. Regis Hotel with the sadist Eleana Soberski on his arm and a Zastava P25 in his ribs. As he and Soberski walked west along K Street, they seemed like the kind of couple not unknown in the neighborhood: a disheveled middle-aged man in a business suit, briefcase swinging at the end of his fist, and an upscale hooker exuding cold impenetrability. Except they were moving away from a four-star hotel rather than toward one for a $500 an hour "date."

Middleton listened for police cruisers' sirens—no doubt the cowering bartender had called the D.C. police who, in turn, would notify the FBI. Lurching along, he wondered if he'd be saved by the people he'd been trying to avoid.

He said, "Where—"

The gun nozzle raked his ribs.

"Farragut Square," Soberski replied, "the statue. Charlotte is there."

Middleton stumbled, but Soberski kept him upright.

"The briefcase," he said.

"Yes, the briefcase," Soberski replied. "Of course, the briefcase. But the briefcase is not enough."

Middleton glanced around. K Street was empty, the sidewalks rolled up now that the dinner hour was through. In New York, Chicago, San Francisco, Krakow, Warsaw, there'd be dozens of people enjoying the night air, on their way to a new hot spot, their chatter and laughter a giddy prelude to what's next. In Washington, you could hear the joyless scrape of the guards' shoes outside Lafayette Park and the White House two blocks away.

"What do you mean 'not enough'?" Middleton asked as they turned north on 16th Street.

"To me, a piece of paper."

"My daughter—"

"Of course you would trade your Chopin for your daughter. But what else?"

They stood at the corner of Connecticut Avenue, pausing as a few taxis headed east. As Middleton caught his breath, he finally heard the wail of sirens, further off than he'd hoped, but drawing nearer.

"There's nothing else," he said. Fatigue clouded his thoughts. The men he'd shot in the bar were after the Chopin manuscript, weren't they?

"Colonel Middleton," she replied with a wry laugh. "Let's not be silly."

"But I don't know what you want."

She jabbed the gun deeper into his ribcage. "Then we will leave it that I know what you want—Charlotte and your grandchild."

Up ahead, the traffic light changed, and Soberski led Middleton off the curb and into the street.

"Anything," he said, as they reached the yellow line.

"Where is Faust?"

A Mercedes sedan eased to the end of the short queue of waiting cars, blocking their path.

"Faust?"

"We are aware of your relationship with Faust," Soberski said.

" 'We'? Who's—"

Before Soberski could react, the driver of the Mercedes jutted his left arm out the open window and squeezed off a shot.

The lone round entered her face at an upward angle, penetrating a nasal bone and exploding the top of her head. Red mist filled the air above Middleton as Soberski collapsed in a heap, the Zastava tumbling from her hand.

"Leave it, Harry."

As sirens blared, Middleton saw his son-in-law staring up at him from behind the wheel of his ex-wife's sedan.

"Leave it and get in. Now Harry."

Seconds later, Jack Perez twisted the wheel and skirted the queue, bursting across the intersection. He raced through a yellow light at George Washington University Hospital, intent on reaching Route 66 before the cops responded to another shooting, this one on Connecticut Avenue.

"Charley?" Middleton asked. The briefcase sat flat on his lap.

"Safe," Perez said, tires squealing as he turned left.

"Sylvia?"

"No, Harry. They got Sylvia."

"Where is—"

"The lake house, Harry. Charley's at the lake house."

Middleton wiped the side of his face, then stared as his bloody palm.

"Before we get there, Harry, you'd better tell me what's going on."

"They're trying to kill me," Middleton managed.

"Trying, but you're not dead," Perez said. "Sylvia, two guys in the bar, two cops at Dulles—"

"Three people in Warsaw," Middleton heard himself say.

"And now the hooker."

"She wasn't—"

"That's nine, and none of them is you."

The ramp up ahead, and what little traffic there was flowed free.

"Jack, listen."

Perez lifted his right hand from the wheel and silently told his father-in-law to keep still. "I just undid a lifetime's worth of work reversing my family's reputation for you, Harry."

Middleton stayed quiet. He knew the Perez family had been connected in the '60s to the

Genovese crime family through Carlo Marcello, but Army Intel said young Jack had tested clean. He never mentioned the off-the-books background check to Charley.

"In return," Perez continued, "you tell me what you're into."

"There's a Chopin manuscript in here," Middleton said, tapping the briefcase's lid. "It's believed to be part of a stash the Nazis squirreled away in a church in Kosovo."

" 'Believed'?"

"It's a forgery. It's not in Chopin's hand. It's been folded, mistreated—"

"And yet somebody thinks it's worth nine lives?"

Middleton remembered the bodies strewn inside St. Sophia, and the dying teenage girl's desperate cry. "Green shirt, green shirt . . . please."

"A lot more than nine, Jack."

They were on the highway now and Perez slid the Mercedes into the fast lane, pushing it up to 70, the sedan riding on a cloud.

"So I'm telling you, Jack, that you and Charley ought to go on thinking I was in Krakow to authenticate—"

"A manuscript that some other expert will know is phony too. Suddenly, you, who's catalogued scores by Bach, Handel, Wagner—"

"Mozart," Middleton added.

"—are fooled by an obvious forgery."

"Jack, what I'm trying to say—"

"And with Charley ready to pop, you go to Poland. That's not you, Harry."

Middleton watched the maple and poplar trees rush by at the roadside. "Are you going to toss that Python?"

Perez had been driving with the .357 pressed against the steering wheel. "Hell no. At least not until you're straight with me."

Middleton sighed. "Better you don't know, Jack."

"Why?" Perez said, peering into the rearview. "You think it's about to get worse?"

Though toughened by a native cynicism and the hardscrabble life of a street musician, 19-year-old Felicia Kaminski was too young to understand that a sense of justice and a blush of optimism raised by an unexpected success were illusions, no more reliable than a promise or a kiss. Still energized by caffeine and the vision of Faust as he was hauled off by airport security, she'd headed from Signor Abe's La Musica shop to an internet café near the Colosseum—another sign of her cleverness: She fled Via delle Botteghe Oscure and hadn't gone to the Pantheon or north to the Trevi Fountain, areas Faust had scouted; nor did she return to her home in San Giovanni. She'd begun to feel she was living a clandestine life, a purposeful life, in memory of her uncle Henryk.

Within the first minute at the computer, she'd

learned Harold Middleton taught "Masterpieces of Music" at the American University in Washington, D.C.

Which was 40 miles—40.23 miles, to be precise—from the address in Baltimore Faust said was to be her new home.

There was a 6:45 flight from Fiumicino through Frankfurt that would arrive in Washington at 12:45. She could exchange her first-class ticket for a coach seat, and still have enough euros—no, dollars—to take a taxi to the college. Even if Professor Middleton was off campus, she could arrange to bring him back—the words "I am Henryk Jedynak's niece" would be enough to earn his attention.

She spent the night in a cheap flop on the Lido, resolute but feeling naked without her violin.

Remembering to use the Joanna Phelps passport Faust had given her, she swapped the ticket at the Alitalia courtesy desk in terminal B, sharing a conspiratorial smile with the young woman behind the counter when she explained that she didn't want to fly with the vecchio sporcaccione—dirty old man—who'd bought it in her name. Incredibly, the woman directed her to retrieve her luggage that had been pulled from yesterday's flight.

Her excuse played with security in baggage claim too, and she returned upstairs to a Lufthansa desk to turn over nearly 1,400 euros for a new ticket. She converted the remaining euros to dollars, paying an exchange rate worthy of a loan shark.

Three hours later, the ample jet was soaring above the Dolomiti on its way to its stopover in Germany. And miracle of miracles, as it departed Frankfurt, the two seats next to her in row 41 remained empty. She slipped off her shoes, grabbed a blanket from an overhead bin and stretched out, her last thoughts a prayer that Middleton would explain everything and a sense that she was about to discover that her uncle had died in defense of art and culture in the form of an unknown composition by Mozart.

She was in a deep sleep, dreaming of music, of a violin with quicksilver strings, of returning to the States—a glimpse of her father, who hadn't appeared to her in years, and the broad-shouldered buildings of Chicago's State Street—when she felt a tug on her toe. She awoke slowly, her mind unable to recall where she was. Opening her eyes, she scrambled to uncoil her body.

"Looking for this?"

Faust held up the oversized envelope that she had seen in Signor Abe's shop. No doubt it contained the Mozart manuscript.

She rose up on her elbows and, to her surprise, spoke in Italian. "Che cosa avete fatto con l'anziano?"

He nudged into the seat on the aisle, and placed a forefinger on his chin. "Old man Nowakowski is fine," he replied in English. "He may continue to be fine."

She stared at him. In a blue-striped business suit, white shirt and a blue tie that matched the sky over the Atlantic, he was utterly composed as he stroked back his long black hair.

"You are very lucky you were not killed last night," he told her.

"It wasn't luck." Her senses had begun to return.

"Well, you were hiding from me, I suppose, which is as good as hiding from them."

"Tell me what's going on."

Faust looked around the rear of the jet. Stewardesses were in the back cabin, preparing the beverage service.

"Think, Joanna," he said. "Your Signor Abe is alive and so are you. I have the Mozart your uncle wanted to protect. Knowing that, tell me how you can believe I am the enemy."

"You say nothing," she said as she sat up, crossing her legs under her. "Niente. Nic. Nothing."

"With the Mozart in my hand, I will go with you to meet Harold Middleton," he replied. "The last man to see your uncle alive—except for the killer, that is."

"You know who killed my uncle?"

Faust stood and held out his hand, beckoning her to leave the narrow row. "Of course," he said, speaking in Polish. "The traitor Vukasin. The lowest of the lows. It's a shame your uncle had to die in his presence."

"Where is he?"

"Vukasin? No doubt he is within a kilometer or so of Colonel Middleton."

Faust turned at the sound of the beverage cart rattling into the aisle.

"Come, Joanna," he said, reaching for her. "They serve Champagne in first class. And Bavarian bleu cheese with a pumpkinseed bread—before lunch. I'm sure the effects of the panzanella and cantucci you had last night have long passed."

Kaminski—no, Phelps—stood and wriggled her feet back into her worn shoes.

The arterial spray from Brocco's severed throat had already dried on his heartbreakingly meager kitchen table, and rigor had begun to subside. Curiously, only his left hand was tied behind his back; his right hung limply, fingertips just above the blood- and urine-stained floor. Tesla saw the outline of a standard-sized reporter's notebook on the table. Which meant the killer coerced Brocco to write something before he died. And getting Brocco to write something meant he was tortured before he was killed.

The killer also recorded Brocco's voice—how else could a dead man call in sick after he died? Clever; a way to buy some time.

But what had he wanted Brocco to write? Tesla

had been asked one pertinent question by Schmidt: Where is Harold Middleton? There are four immediate answers Brocco could have given: Middleton's true location; a false one; a concession that he didn't know where he was—as Tesla had—or a refusal to say anything. All but the first would lead to escalating pain and, if Brocco hadn't known where his old boss was, he could have been compelled into speculation.

Tesla looked at her former colleague and, though his head was lolled back and his eyes opened wide and empty, she remembered tenderly his earnestness, his awkwardness around women, his passion for 18th century classical music, his unassailable belief in the power of a free press.

She peered into his mouth and saw that his tongue had been cut out. Which explained the dried blood on his lips and chin, and also whatever he wrote on the notebook's page.

Tesla went to the sink to retrieve a ratty dishtowel, and brought it to the old, newsprint-smudged yellow wall phone. She dialed 911, gave them Brocco's address and then let the handset fall, the towel unraveling and landing on the worn linoleum.

As she turned to leave, she saw Brocco had five deadbolt locks on the door. His tattered khaki saddlebag, which hung from the knob, was empty.

The ultra-cautious Brocco had let the killer in. The killer stole Brocco's laptop.

Brocco knew the killer, and the email addresses stored in the laptop weren't enough.

Tesla hustled down three flights of stairs and stepped into the late-afternoon sun. Shaken, her thoughts occupied by Brocco's brutal murder as well as by speculation on where Harold might be, she momentarily abandoned the vigilance she applied when she stepped off the Acela in Wilmington, only to taxi to BWI, scurry through the airport as if she were late for a flight, and then pop back on Amtrak to Union Station, buying a ticket using a credit card issued to a woman who worked as an extra at Il Teatro Constanzi in Rome. Now as she hurried to catch the Georgia Avenue bus as it wheezed from its stop, she suddenly remembered, with a startling vividness, an unexpectedly satisfying afternoon she'd spent with Harold at a house on Lake Anna. Were she the type to blush, she would've.

Lake Anna, she told herself, unaware that she'd failed to see a man in an old sun-baked Citröen sitting directly across from Brocco's shabby building. He wore a black stocking cap atop his shaved head; the cap covered a black-and-green tattoo of the jack of spades.

When Tesla leaped onto the bus, the man turned the ignition key, folded the switchblade he'd been using to clean his fingernails, and eased the car out of the spot.

He was waiting when, 33 minutes later, the

woman in black pulled out of the Budget lot at Union Station in a dark blue rental, sunglasses on her nose.

There was nothing else they could do. They had no choice.

The Mercedes had kicked up pebbles as Perez parked it at the side of the house. As Middleton hoisted his weary body from the car, Perez said, "Harry, no lights."

"She's sleeping?"

"Harry . . ."

No, of course not. Charley sent her husband to "Scotland" to rescue her father. If she wasn't pregnant, she'd have been there herself.

Perez pulled the Python.

Groping through darkness, they'd stepped inside the house, and as Perez climbed the stairs to the bedrooms, Middleton put down his briefcase and headed through the kitchen to the living room.

Through the picture window, he saw his daughter's silhouette on the porch. She was slumped in a wicker chair.

"Charley," he'd whispered. Then he said her name again, louder this time.

When she didn't respond, Middleton called to his son-in-law and raced outside.

Charley had his Browning A-Bolt across her lap.

Beneath the wicker chair was a tiny puddle of blood that had been dripping from between her legs.

Middleton recoiled.

"Oh Jesus," Perez said as he skidded to a halt. "Charley. Charley, wake up."

At that moment, Middleton understood that his daughter had lost her baby. He felt a muted sense of relief: For a moment, seeing the blood, he thought they had gotten to her as they had Henryk Jedynak, Sylvia and others—and had tried to kill him at Dulles.

Kneeling, Perez said, "She needs—"

"Yeah, she does."

And now Charlotte Perez was recovering at Martha Jefferson Hospital. A private room, IV drip in place, and her husband at her side, barely awake in a lounge chair with a .357 Magnum in his jacket side pocket.

Honey sunlight streamed through the windows. Treetops swayed in the gentle breeze.

Felt like hiding in plain sight to Harold Middleton.

To Jack Perez too.

11

PETER SPIEGELMAN

Felicia Kaminski collapsed on the vast sofa that sat before the window that filled the wall of a suite atop the Harbor Court Hotel. The fat, silk-covered cushions nearly swallowed her whole. Far below, the lights of Baltimore's Inner Harbor blinked yellow and white at her, and big boats bobbed like eggs on the black water. Was there something in the blinking lights—some pattern, a signal, a message meant for her? If there was, she was too tired to decipher it.

Beyond tired, really. She was spent—exhausted by fear and flight, and addled by too many time zones and Champagne that flowed freely in the first-class cabin. Faust had all but forced it on her, and he'd kept up with her glass for glass, all the while smiling like the Cheshire Cat. One bottle had led to another—so many bubbles—but the smiling Mr. Faust seemed entirely immune.

Kaminski closed her eyes, but she could still see his white teeth and those dark, stony eyes, could still hear that deep melodious voice speaking in Italian, then in French, in Polish, in German, and now in English as he addressed the hotel man. There was a rueful smile in his words. Without looking, she knew that the hotel man—not a bellman but the immaculate, blue-suited fellow from behind the desk—was smiling back and nodding. It was all smiles and nods and discreet bows for Mr. Faust, all along the way: on the airplane; in the executive lounge in Frankfurt as they waited to fly to the States; and from the man at Dulles who met them, retrieved their luggage and drove them in a shiny black BMW all the way to Baltimore. It was as if they all knew him, their oldest friend, dear Mr. Faust—who smiled and drank Champagne and spoke in many tongues, but answered questions in none of them.

Kaminski sighed and sank deeper into the cushions. Her head swam and the harbor lights blinked at her, even through her closed lids. She had smoked opium once, an oily black bead with that Tunisian boy—what was his name?—who played guitar near the Castel Sant'Angelo, and it had set her drifting like this. Floating, her worries no more than distant lights.

There was a sharp knock and she came to with a bump. She rubbed her eyes and sat up to see Faust opening the suite door. A man came in, squat and muscular, wearing jeans and a black-leather jacket. His hair was gray and cut short, and he greeted Faust in Italian, then glanced at his guest and switched to something else. Whatever it was sounded fast and harsh to Kaminski's ears— Slavic, she thought, but otherwise no clue. Faust listened and nodded and checked his watch. He said something to the man—an order, a dismissal—and the man nodded and left.

Faust looked at her. "Another trip," he said.

Felicia could barely find her voice. "What? Now? At this hour?"

Again the smile. "No rest for the wicked, Felicia, but we won't be gone long. If you wish to wash up first, I will wait."

She rubbed her hands over her face, rubbing life back into it. "No," she said. "I'm tired of being dragged around, and now I'm done with it. Sono rifinito. Non sto andando."

Even to herself she sounded like a child, but she was beyond caring. She looked at Faust, leaning so casually against the doorframe, his suit somehow without a wrinkle and every hair in place, as if he had stepped from a page in a fashion magazine.

He shook his head. "You are not staying here alone, Felicia."

Anger welled in her. "No? And why not?"

"It is not safe."

"I take care of myself."

"Yes, I saw how well back in Rome."

She said, "Screw you! I don't need a goddamn babysitter."

"You are the tough little urchin now, eh?"

"Tough enough," Kaminski said, grinding her teeth. "I didn't grow up in places like this, being waited on hand and foot."

Faust's smile widened. "You think that I did?"

"Let's say you don't look out of place."

He chuckled. "You haven't known the real romance of street life until you've experienced it in Buenos Aires, caught between the Montoneros and the Battalion 601 boys. Now those were charming fellows, and much more dedicated than your average Roman teppista."

Kaminski massaged her temples, trying to get her brain to function. Buenos Aires? Montoneros? What the fuck? She'd read something once about the Dirty War, but she couldn't remember what. "So you had it rough and now you're up from the gutter—a real success story."

"Something like that."

"Good for you. You've earned all this! And never mind that you're a thief or a spy or some kind of terrorist—someone who bullies old men, and kidnaps girls from the streets of Rome."

"I've told you, Felicia, your friend Abe is fine, and I am no spy. I have no taste for politics at all. If I had to describe my profession, I'd say I was a broker. I match buyers with sellers, and take a fee. A modest fee, all things considered."

"Buyers and sellers of what?"

Faust shrugged. "This and that. Odds and ends."

"Like stolen music manuscripts?"

"The manuscript is in the closet, Felicia, behind lock and key. My own musical inclinations run more to Sinatra than Mozart."

171

"Not music, then what—drugs, guns? Whatever it is, I'm sure it makes your family very proud."

Kaminski felt the air change, going silent and thick around her. The smiling Mr. Faust was no longer smiling, and those dark eyes seemed to look right through her. Defiance and anger drained from her, replaced by choking fear. This time, the knock on the door was a relief.

It was the squat man again, and he looked nervously at Faust. Faust said something to the man—she didn't know what—and walked out the door. The squat man turned to her.

"Come," he said in gravelly English.

She was not inclined to argue.

Faust hadn't lied about the trip. It was a short one in the back of the big BMW, through sodium-lit nighttime streets. Kaminski looked for signs and landmarks: Light Street, East Lombard, a big stadium off to the left, bathed in light and carpeted in impossible green, then a tangle of narrower streets, and old brick buildings. In 10 minutes, they pulled up in front of one of them.

Four stories and broad, the building looked to her like a warehouse or an old factory. And so it had been once upon a time, as she read on the shiny brass plaque near the modern glass entry: The Sail Cloth Factory—1888. Just above that plaque another, with the address: 121 South Fremont Avenue.

Home, she thought, her anger returning as she followed Faust inside.

Exposed brick and ornamental wrought iron whispered of the building's industrial past; otherwise, the rest of the lobby—gleaming brass, etched glass and marble—proclaimed its current incarnation as a luxury apartment building. Faust crossed to the elevator and Felicia followed him in and then, on the fourth floor, out again. Around a corner, down a pale gray corridor, and to a black door at its end; Faust knocked twice. Then he took a key from his jacket pocket, worked the lock, and stepped inside. And stopped short.

Kaminski didn't see the wiry, bearded man pointing a Glock 30 at Faust's chest until she bumped into Faust's back. Then she gasped and gripped Faust's bicep.

"Jesus," she whispered.

The bearded man smiled at Faust, who smiled back. "*Qué tal*, Nacho," Faust said.

"*Nada*, Jefe," the man said, and slipped the Glock into a holster behind his back. "All quiet on the western front. Have a look for yourself."

Faust gently removed Kaminski's hand from his bicep and followed Nacho to a window. She let out a long breath and looked around. The large loft apartment—brick walls, high ceilings, exposed beams and ductwork, shiny plank floors, and little in the way of furniture: a card table, some folding chairs, a dim floor lamp, and heavy white drapes across the windows. There was plenty of technical equipment: three laptops; several cameras wearing long lenses; and two massive, tripod-mounted binoculars. They were pointed at a narrow gap in the drapes, and now Nacho fiddled with one of them.

"Got the image intensifier on this one, Jefe," he said as Faust bent to the eyepieces.

"When was the last delivery?" Faust asked as he looked.

"This afternoon. Maybe five o'clock."

"You know what it was?"

Nacho looked at Kaminski and switched to Spanish. She tried to follow it, but it came too fast and the accents were strange, and anyway it sounded scientific to her, chemical terms maybe. She walked slowly to the binoculars while Faust and Nacho spoke. The men saw her but seemed not to care. She peered into the eyepiece.

Outside, the world was tinted green, as was a brick building, low and long, that seemed very close. It had a lot of windows, all shuttered, and she thought it looked abandoned. There was a loading dock in the center of the image, and the only thing that moved was a plastic bag, blowing in the warm night breeze.

Nacho pulled the drapes and the outside images went black. He looked at Kaminski and nodded his head at a chair in the corner. She sat, still straining to catch the conversation. It was less technical

now, Faust asking something about someone—
does he know . . . Does he know what? Horario.
Was that like orario, meaning schedule, timetable?
And who was this he?

It seemed as if Nacho was uncertain too. He
shrugged at Faust and moved to a large closet's
double doors. He put his hands on the knobs.
"Maybe you have better luck than me, Jefe," he
said in English, and swung the doors wide.

Kaminski screamed.

The man on the closet floor stared at her, though
he was bound with wire and gagged with duct tape,
and bleeding from a gash on his shaved head,
which, she noticed, was tattooed with the likeness
of the jack of spades. Nacho pressed a forefinger to
his lips and made a shushing noise at her.

She had no idea how long it was before her head
cleared, but when it did she saw Faust kneeling by
the tattooed man. His hand rested gently on the
man's shoulder, and he spoke softly in his ear. The
duct tape was off the tattooed man's mouth and
Kaminski could see that the man's lips were split,
and that he was crying. And speaking too, in
urgent, terrified English.

"No, no—not weeks! It's days, a matter of days.
Maybe less!"

Faust spread the duct tape over the man's mouth
again and patted him, almost affectionately, on the
back. Then he stepped away and shut the closet
door. Nacho looked at Faust and smiled.

"Still got the touch, Jefe," he said.

Faust smiled minutely. "You call if there's any more activity," he said. To Kaminski, he added, "We return to the hotel."

She stood and followed numbly. As they were about to step into the corridor, she touched Faust's arm and spoke in a whisper. "What will happen to him—the man in the closet?"

"Nacho will see to him," Faust said. "Now come, we have dinner plans to make."

It was nearly black in the hospital room when Jack Perez came awake, the .357 in his hand. The only light came from the orange glow of the call buttons on the wall, the green digits on the blood pressure monitor, and the pinkish scatter of streetlight through the shaded window. It was nearly silent, too—only the sounds of his wife's steady breathing, the quiet whir of air in the vents, and the electric ping of some sort of warning bell reached his ears. About right for two a.m.

But something had woken Perez from his brittle sleep. His father-in-law going out? Someone in the corridor?

Perez wiped a hand across his eyes, rose from the lounge chair and crossed the room without a sound. He leaned against the doorframe with one hand on the knob and the .357 down along his leg. He took a deep breath and opened the door a crack.

Middleton was down the hall, his back to Perez,

and he was talking quietly to a man and a woman. The man was lanky and pale, and his jaw was darkened by a three-day beard. His eyes were shadowed and darting. The woman was tall, tanned, and broad-shouldered, and her dark hair was cut short. Perez hadn't made a sound, but somehow Middleton knew he was there.

"Come meet some old friends, Jack," he said, without turning around. Perez pocketed the Python and closed the door to his wife's room behind him.

"This is Jean-Marc Lespasse and Leonora Tesla, former colleagues of mine. Nora, JM, this is my son-in-law, Jack Perez."

Lespasse nodded at Perez, and Tesla put out a warm hand. "Harry has told us all that's happened, Mr. Perez. I'm so sorry for what you and your wife have been through. Will she be all right?"

"She's lost a lot of blood, but the docs say she'll recover. All right is another story. I don't know that either one of us will be all right again after this."

As Tesla nodded sympathetically, Middleton said, "Nora and JM have been through the wringer themselves the past couple of days. A man nearly killed Nora in Namibia, and JM narrowly avoided abduction in Chapel Hill."

"Jesus, Harry, is all this about—?"

"We think so," Middleton said. "The man who attacked Nora was looking for me."

"I didn't hang around to find out what those

clowns in the parking lot were after," Lespasse added in a raspy whisper, "but I heard them speaking Serbian, and they were carrying those cheap shit Zastavas."

"And this is all about . . . what? That fucking manuscript?" Perez asked.

Tesla and Lespasse shifted nervously. Middleton said nothing.

"For Christ's sakes, Harry . . ." Perez said, shaking his head. He looked at Tesla. "How did you two manage to find us?"

"We both saw the news reports of Harry's difficulty at Dulles and knew that he was . . . in flight. We both guessed that he might turn up at the lake house."

"I ran into Nora there," Lespasse said.

". . . and nearly blew my head off."

"We saw the blood and thought the worst," Lespasse added. "We started checking hospitals, closest ones first, and there you were."

Perez turned back to his father-in-law. "Not too difficult. And the guys who are after you, whoever they are, seem fuckin' relentless. How much longer before they turn up here too?"

Any answer Middleton might have given was interrupted by the night duty nurse. "You and your father-in-law will have to quiet down, Mr. Perez, and your friends will have to come back during regular visiting hours."

Middleton seized the opportunity. "Yes, ma'am,

and we're very sorry. I'll just see these folks out so Jack can sit with Charley."

He took Tesla's arm and led her and Jean-Marc toward the elevator, leaving Jack Perez grinding his teeth in the darkened hallway.

Outside, the air was warm and close. The hospital parking lot was nearly empty. Jean-Marc Lespasse lit a cigarette, inhaled deeply, and blew a column of smoke into the night sky.

Harry Middleton recalled the last time he'd seen Lespasse and Val Brocco. A blisteringly hot day at chaotic Kenyatta Airport. He remembered too his farewell to Nora Tesla. It had been somewhat after his final meeting with the two men and the location was much nicer—an Algerian-influenced inn on the Cote D'Azure—but the moment was no less difficult.

Events intervened . . .

She glanced at him once and then her eyes fled. Words seemed easier.

"Your family has no idea?" Leonora Tesla asked Middleton.

"No. I never told them—never thought I'd have to. I thought I could protect them from . . . all this."

She clutched his hand, an instinctive gesture, and released it fast. "This isn't your fault, Harry, but your son-in-law is right. It wasn't difficult for us to find you, and it won't be difficult for anyone else who's looking. It's not safe."

"It's safe enough for a little while—long enough for me to think things through. The Soberski woman asked about Faust. She thought I was into something with him."

"So you said, Harry, and I told you, Eleana Soberski was a sociopath and a congenital liar," Tesla said. "You have to assume that anything she said was meant to mislead and to manipulate. Faust was our boogeyman—our white whale—and she knew that. What better way to get your attention than dangle his name?"

"She didn't have to dangle anything, Nora. She had a gun in my ribs."

Blowing out more smoke, Lespasse said, "She thought she was going to be interrogating you, Harry. She was laying groundwork, putting you off balance. She—"

Before Lespasse could finish, Middleton's cell phone burred. He found it in a pocket, flipped it open and heard only static. And then a faraway voice, old and struggling in English.

"Colonel Middleton? My name is Abraham Nowakowski. I'm calling from Rome and I have a message from Felicia Kaminski—Henryk Jedynak's niece. An urgent message."

Harold Middleton listened intently for several minutes. Then he said, "Ciao, Signor Abe, mille grazie." Closing his phone, he let out a massive breath. Tesla and Lespasse looked at him expectantly.

"Speak of the devil, and the devil appears," Middleton said. "Faust. He's in the country, and close—up in Baltimore. He's got something Henryk Jedynak was holding for me, and he's got Jedynak's niece too."

"Baltimore? What the hell is he doing in Baltimore?" Lespasse asked.

"I don't know. Jedynak's niece managed to get a call out to a family friend in Rome—that's who was on the line. From what he said, it sounds like Faust has some sort of operation going on there, but the girl was cut off after a minute."

"Did she say where in Baltimore Faust is?" Tesla asked.

"No, but she did tell her friend where she and Faust would be tomorrow—check that—tonight. A place called Kali's Court, on Thames Street. Apparently the two of them are going there for dinner. Just the two of them. I'm thinking that maybe we should join them."

Tesla and Lespasse looked at Middleton. Tesla shook her head. "Join them? You can't be serious, Harry—with only three of us."

"We need backup for something like that, Colonel," Lespasse said. "Unless what you want is in and out, bang, bang, bang."

Middleton shook his head. "That's appealing, but not smart. No, we need to talk to this guy, and at length. So backup it is." Harry opened his phone again and clicked through his list of con-

181

tacts. He stopped on an entry marked E.K. and hit dial.

The phone rang once.

The voice in Middleton's ear said, "It's about time you called, Harry. But then I guess you've had your hands full lately."

"I need a team, Emmett," Middleton said. "In Baltimore."

"Sure you do, Harry. And what about what I need?"

"We can talk about that too, after we settle Baltimore."

"We can fuckin' talk about it now.

"It's been real bad luck for people to run into you lately, Harry. We've got bodies at Dulles, downtown on Sixteenth Street and two assholes with fake Bureau IDs in a bar nearby. Okay, sure, self-defense. But you still have to answer questions. And we can't stop the local boys from bringing you in if they find out. Jesus, you should've told us from the beginning what was going on."

"Guess what, Emmett. Somebody forgot to send me an agenda. I didn't know what was going on. And I still don't."

"Be that as it may, we need to talk."

"No time, Emmett. My battery's running low."

"Not to worry, Harry, we can talk about it over coffee. Say in five minutes, in the hospital cafeteria." Middleton looked left, right, overhead. On the phone Kalmbach laughed nastily. "On your left," he said. "Across the street."

Middleton peered into the darkness and a pair of headlights of a Bureau-issued car winked once, twice at him. Emmett Kalmbach was still laughing. "Cream and two sugars for me, Harry."

In his suite at the Harbor Court Hotel, the man known as Faust answered the muted beep of a cell phone. The voice on the other end was faraway and old. Faust listened intently, and a small, satisfied smile played on his lips. "Well done, Signor Abe," he said.

Faust put his phone down and looked across the sitting room, into the smaller of the suite's two bedrooms. A splash of light fell across the king-sized bed, and in it he could see Kaminski's pale face on the pillow, and a spray of blond hair.

"Charming," he said again, to no one in particular.

12

RALPH PEZZULLO

There was something about Fells Point that put Harold Middleton in a foul mood. Maybe it had to do with the fight at The Horse You Came In Saloon that got him booted out of West Point. Maybe it related to the scar on his left temple left by a bar stool—the one that still throbbed whenever the thermometer dipped below 40.

This dank place changed my life, he thought, entering the fog that clung like bad luck to Baltimore's Thames Street.

Charley's miscarriage; his ex-wife Sylvia's violent death; the mayhem and destruction that trailed him since the meeting in Krakow: Now he was determined to right all that, coming on like St. George to slay the dragon as in the richly colored depiction by Raphael Sanzio he admired, even if Faust had chosen Kali's Court in some sort of a sick cosmic joke. He smiled to himself. Wasn't Kali the Hindu goddess of annihilation?

As he peered through the fog, Middleton reminded himself to focus. The forces aligned against him were vile and dark. The equation he followed was simple. He had come to slay evil, which had manifested in numbing complexity.

Nora Tesla's voice squawked in his earpiece. "Target's in. Alone."

That's strange, he thought, marching over the same cobblestones he'd been tossed to like trash so many years ago. "Kaminski isn't with him?"

"I said, 'Alone.'"

So you did. Middleton pushed his shoulders back, fixed the collar of his coat and entered the restaurant. A hostess with a frosted smile stopped him with hard blue eyes. "You have a reservation?"

"I'm meeting someone. A man. Mid-thirties, long dark hair, slicked back, tall. Just arrived . . ."

"I know him. Yes." Suddenly flummoxed, she managed to smile and frown at the same time. "He said he was dining alone."

"Not tonight, my dear."

Middleton's Dover Saddlery riding boots reverberated confidently across the walnut floor past Tesla and Lespasse in a nearby booth, along with an FBI agent and another man, ambiguously titled, but one whose job became clearer if you knew his phone number was an exchange near Crystal City, Virginia, the home of the Pentagon.

Outside, in a control van, were some other distinguished visitors: Emmett Kalmbach and Homeland Security's Richard Chambers.

Such seniority at a surveillance operation was unusual. But Faust was such a wild card, and the recent shootings so troubling, that both the major agencies responsible for tracking foreign threats within the U.S. wanted direct involvement. Middleton knew Kalmbach. The man could be spineless, but Middleton didn't care; all the easier to get what he wanted from the feebies on Ninth Street. As for Dick Chambers, the regional director wouldn't have much personal interest in Faust. The politics of the Balkans hadn't intrigued him. He'd made one trip to the region during the conflicts, apparently deemed it solvable by underlings and headed off for the Middle East—where he saw more of a threat to the U.S., about which he was right, of course.

But Chambers's presence here could be explained by a simpler reason: The DHS, the organization that brought us the color-coded threat levels and was charged with protecting our borders, had screwed up big time and, focused on people who's last names began with al-, had missed Vukasin, a known war criminal, and an unknown number of his goons sneaking into the country on phony papers.

Which wasn't necessarily bad news for Middleton. It meant that Chambers needed to protect his image and could bring resources to bear in a big way. Middleton was confident that all the pieces were in place for checkmate.

Spotting thick black eyebrows protruding over the top of the Racing Form, Middleton stopped and lowered his chin. "Good evening, Faust," he said deeply, placing the edge of his briefcase on the table. His heart was beating fast, palms moist. The man he'd been tracking for years was now in front of him. He seemed diminished, much smaller than Middleton expected, though he knew the physical details of the war criminal better than he knew his own.

"I rather liked Patty's Special in the eighth running ten to one," came the reply. Faust set down the paper and smoothed it carefully. "Colonel Harold Middleton."

The swarthy-skinned man with the lopsided grin looked up briefly, then snapped his fingers at the nervous waiter with the puff of blond hair. "Bring a glass for my friend." Then to Middleton, he said, "I hope you don't mind Beaujolais."

The American beamed at his quarry's attempt at gamesmanship. "I have you, Faust," he said as he pulled out a chair and sat. "We can do this anyway you want."

Faust folded the paper and fixed him with intense black eyes. " 'Unhappy master, who unmerciful disaster followed fast and followed faster, till his songs the burden bore; till the dirges of his hope, the melancholy burden bore of Nevermore, of Nevermore.' "

"I deplore people who play with other people's lives."

"So do I."

"It's over."

"Let's hope not, Colonel." The man took a bite of food, which he seemed to relish. He then said, "One thing I've never thanked you for. My name."

"Your name?"

"That was your creation. I believe you found some documents in a volume of Goethe's masterpiece, and dubbed me after the hero."

"You think Faust was a hero?"

"Protagonist then." He raised his glass. "So here's to selling our souls to the devil."

Middleton let his wine glass sit, untouched.

They confronted each other's stare. Middleton wanted nothing more than to reach over and wring the younger man's neck.

Faust said, "The great Edgar Allen Poe died at Church Hospital, very close to here. Few grieved. The poor mad genius was placed in an unmarked grave. His last words: 'Lord help my soul.'"

"It seems you identify with him."

Faust shook his head. "I was thinking he was more like you. Condemned to walk the earth as a marked man. Walking down the avenue of life stalked by demons. Using his will to bend his torment into art."

Middleton drank down his wine then slammed his fist onto the table. "You're a criminal! A fiend! I still dream about the slaughtered children of Kosovo and Racak."

Faust laughed into his fist, adding fire to Middleton's anger. Then he held up his hand.

"Easy, my friend. Why it is that you Americans always assume that everything is black and white?"

"In this case, it is."

"So if it has a pink ribbon tied around it it's a birthday present?"

"Maybe you didn't pull the trigger yourself, but you backed the man who did."

"Rugova was a pig. May he rest in—"

"I hope he's rotting in hell."

"He was useful."

Middleton stabbed a finger toward his rival's chin. "You stink of guilt."

"I like you, Colonel. I need you. That's why I must stop you from continuing to demean your own intelligence."

Before Middleton could reply, Faust snapped his fingers at the waiter, who skittered across the dining room. "My guest here will have the lacquered octopus to start; for me, the pear and caramelized walnut salad. We'd both like the whole Bronzini. No salt."

Faust lifted his glass. "Here's to the beginning of our partnership. Success!"

"What the hell are you talking about?"

"Tens of thousands; maybe hundreds of thousands of people are counting on us, but don't know it."

"Music lovers?" he asked darkly.

"I know a great deal about you, Colonel. I've

studied you carefully. You're a man who is relentless in pursuit of what you consider a worthy goal. I hope you'll excuse me if I say that your goals so far have been wrong-headed."

The salad and octopus arrived and were soon treated to showers of fresh black pepper.

"I bet you the price of this meal that we'll be working together by the evening's end," Faust offered.

Middleton nodded his acceptance.

In a small bookkeeper's office in a corner of the lemon-and-brine-scented kitchen of Kali's Court, M. T. Connolly sat listening with desperate attention to the two men at the table not 50 yards from her, their voices traveling through an earbud.

Kalmbach. At his disposal were hundreds of Bureau agents and yet, in a display of typically unnecessary bravado, he drove to Martha Jefferson Hospital by himself, unaware Connolly was behind him. Now, hours later, Kalmbach, with Dick Chambers in tow, had led her to Middleton. And Faust, who was beginning the next phase of his dissertation with an anecdote about his father.

Connolly listened hard. The bug was under Faust's bread plate.

". . . Invitations to dance made with simple nods," Faust said. "The intense courtship . . ."

She jumped as her cell phone rang. She stretched

her leg and snapped it quickly from her belt. "This is Connolly."

"Hello, Buttercup."

She walked toward a corner, away from the kitchen staff's prying eyes. "Padlo," she said, her voice barely above a whisper. "Where are you?"

"Sono a Roma," he replied, his Italian accented with as much American English as his native Polish. "Someone wants to say hello."

"Josef, wait—"

"Oh, and by the way, his English is . . . Actually, it's non-existent."

Connolly sighed as Faust and Middleton continued in her other ear.

"Buona sera, Signora Connolly," an old man said nervously. "Il mio nome è Abe Nowakowski. Posso aiutarlo con il vostro commercio."

"I'm sorry—'Commercio'? I don't—"

"Business," Padlo said, taking the heavy black handset in the old man's shop. "Which is still finding Middleton, I presume."

"I've got Middleton," Padlo heard her say. "And Faust."

When Padlo repeated the names, the old man recoiled.

"They are together?" Padlo asked.

"Together, and negotiating."

Nowakowski, who had lived in terror since the moment he first saw the Mozart score, said, "Dove è il Felicia?"

Padlo saw that the old man trembled. "A young girl," the deputy said to Connolly. "Felicia Kaminski. Jedynak's niece." Recalling her photo, he began to describe her.

"She's not here," Connolly said.

"Harbor Court," the old man told Padlo.

Padlo repeated the hotel's name.

Not now, Connolly thought as she shut her cell phone.

Out in the dining room, Faust had made his play.

Faust said, "My father was a relatively old man when he married my mother. They met at a type of tango bar we call milangas in Buenos Aires. A scratchy Carlos Gardel record, seductive glances filled with subverted desire. Invitations to dance made with simple nods. The intense courtship begins with toe-tangling turns and kicks under crystal chandeliers. Before they speak, it seems to my father that they're making love."

"What's your father got to do with this?"

"As a young man, my father was a chemist in Poland. He said my mother reminded him of his first wife, a gypsy, Zumella. She died in Europe during the war."

"Along with million and millions of others. If we didn't stop that madman we'd all be speaking German."

"He called my mother Jolanta—violet blossom. He was a sentimental man. He met his first wife selling violet blossoms in Castle Square in Warsaw."

"I fail to see what this—"

"Colonel Middleton, in all your travels or investigations for the government have you ever heard the name Projekt 93?"

"I don't believe I have."

"Are you familiar with the work of Gerhard Schrader?"

Middleton shook his head.

"A German chemist who experimented with chemical agents. He invented Tabun, which was originally used to kill insects, then adapted as a lethal weapon against mankind. The Nazis produced twelve-thousand tons of the stuff at a secret plant in Poland, code named Hockwerk."

Faust dipped into a briefcase at his feet and removed a photocopy of a document from the Nuremberg Tribunal. "My father worked at Hockwerk. His name is fourth on this list."

"Kazimierz Rymut?"

"You'll note the asterisk, which refers to the footnote at the bottom. It might be hard to read so I'll quote it for you: 'This individual has been exculpated due to cooperation he provided regarding experiments conducted on human subjects.'"

"I'm not sure I know what that means."

"It means that my father heard that some of the chemical agents he was working on—agents that he assumed would be used to kill rats and other rodents—were being used on human beings. On October 14, 1944, Doctor Josef Mengele removed approximately five thousands gypsies from Sachsenhausen concentration camp outside Oranienberg and had them trucked into a wooded area near Rudna, Poland. There they were sprayed with Sarin gas. Within hours, every single man, woman and child died."

"Isn't that the same material that was used in the subway attack in Tokyo?"

"By the Aum Shinrikyo cult. Yes."

Faust's hand drifted toward his briefcase. "I have in my possession the official report, but will spare you the details. Suffice it to say, the results were ghastly. When rumors of this event reached my father, I'm sure he refused to believe them at first. He was a man, like many, who tried to insulate himself from the ugliness of the world around him. He listened to Vivaldi, tinkered with coo-coo clocks, baked pastries, wept at the faces of young children. He was not like us, Colonel. And yet when confronted with the horror of what was going on around him, he acted."

Middleton said, "Sounds like your father was a hero."

"He became a hero and a great example to me. I won't go into all the details of what he did except to say that he found a way to pass details of the chemical weapon program at Hockwerk known as Projekt 93 to the Allies, which helped them target the plant before it could cause any more damage."

"Thank God."

The waiter arrived with the Bronzini, which gave off a faint scent of orange blossom under a delicate brown crust.

"Yes, thank God," Faust said as he sampled the fish, deeming it delightful. "The maniacs were stopped. But evil men have a way of rediscovering the most horrifying things."

Middleton nodded. "I do believe that evil is an active force in the world."

Faust leaned closer and almost whispered, "And you and I are going to stop it."

"How?" Middleton was confused. A part of him wanted to believe Faust; another part was hugely skeptical. "I still don't understand how this relates to us, here, tonight."

"Because, Colonel, some of the manuscripts that you found hidden in St. Sophia, in the Czartoryski Collection, were not about music. This is what your friend Henryk Jedynak was on the verge of telling you. That's why he was killed."

"Why?"

"Because encrypted in the musical notes are formulas for a number of V-agents—highly stable nerve agents that were developed at Hockwerk, many times more lethal that Sarin or Tabun. The most potent of these is known as VX. Scientists call it the most toxic synthesized compound known to man."

"If this is true—"

"It's undoubtedly true! I'll provide the supporting documents," Faust said. "I assume you'll thoroughly check out the story yourself."

"Of course."

"The clock is ticking, Colonel. We don't have much time."

"Why?"

"I don't think I need to tell you which formula is encrypted into the Chopin manuscript."

"VX."

"Correct."

Middleton's mind worked feverishly, tracking back over all that had happened since he first saw the manuscripts in Pristina.

Faust tore into a piece of bread. "Vukasin must be stopped!"

"The Wolf is behind all this?" He thought of Sylvia, his ex; and Charley, who was still at risk.

"Absolutely. His plan is horrifying. Unimaginably cruel."

"But Rugova . . . Where did he fit in?"

"Sometimes one doesn't have the luxury to choose the most favorable allies. When I learned about the existence of the manuscripts, I hired Rugova to help me. He wasn't particularly reliable or sympathetic. I was, I regret to say, desperate. I'm even more desperate now."

• • •

Vukasin knew he was alone now—alone amid perhaps five police cruisers, nine uniformed cops and maybe twice as many in plainclothes who had come to the Martha Jefferson Hospital. Someone had been smart: They had told local law enforcement that Middleton, the man they believed had killed two policemen at Dulles, had been spotted at the hospital and would soon return. So right now Charlotte Middleton-Perez was as protected as anyone inside the Beltway. She could not be Vukasin's next victim. Too bad, he thought. He would have to draw out Middleton in some other way.

And he would have to do it. Andrzej, his last reliable agent in the States, had failed to contact him after trailing the Volunteer Tesla from the house at Lake Anna to who knows where; Vukasin imagined the killer and his shaved head, with its ridiculous jack of spades tattoo, had been served to pigs in the countryside. Soberski had failed too—getting her head blown off in the middle of the street a short walk from the White House. Briefly, he wondered what the sadist's last utterance had been.

Well, Vukasin thought, as he retreated in the forest behind the hospital. With all the work comes all the honor. Tens of thousands of dead Americans, and the credit will belong only to me.

But one last chore.

The Harbor Court Hotel, near the next Ground Zero, was only 150 or so miles north. Driving with caution, he'd be there in four hours.

He smiled at the thought of what would occur after he arrived.

13

LISA SCOTTOLINE

Charley Middleton-Perez floated in that netherworld between wakefulness and sleep, anxiety tugging at the edge of her consciousness like a toddler at the hem of his mother's skirt. She knew at some vague level that she was in a hospital room, that her husband Jack was asleep in the chair beside her, and that the doctors had given her meds to help her rest. From outside in the hall came the faint rattle of a cart gliding over a polished floor and people talking in low voices. She didn't care enough to eavesdrop. She remained in the drug cocoon, pharmaceutically insulated from her fears.

Unfortunately, it was wearing off. And no drug could quell these fears, not forever. So much had happened, almost all at once. In her mind's eye, she saw the scenes flicker backward in time, a gruesome rewind. Someone had tried to kill her. They'd murdered her mother, and she had seen her dead on the floor, her lovely features contorted and a blackening pool of blood beneath her head, seeping into the grains of the oak floor, filling its lines like a grisly etching.

Troubled, shifting in the bed, she flashed on her father running for his life. And her husband Jack had risked everything to save them both.

But there was one life he couldn't save.

She heard a slight moan and realized that it came from her. She was waking up, though she wasn't sure she wanted to. Closer to wakefulness than sleep, she felt an emptiness that she realized was literally true. She was empty now.

The baby was gone. The baby she had carried for the past five months, within her very body.

She had loved being pregnant, every minute of it. They had tried for the baby for so long, and she couldn't believe when they'd finally gotten pregnant. She'd memorized baby books, and from day one of her pregnancy, was mindful that every spoonful she put into her mouth and every sip of every drink, she was taking for them both. She ate plain yogurt, gave up her beloved chocolate, fled from secondhand smoke and refused anti-nausea meds when her morning sickness was its worst. Her every thought had been to nurture the baby, one they'd both wanted so much.

Jack, Jr.

She had decided to name him Jack, Jr., and Jack would have loved the idea. Now she would never tell him her plan. He hadn't wanted to know whether the baby was a boy or a girl, so she'd kept it from him too, though she was bursting with the news.

Surprise me, he had said, the night she had found out, a smile playing around his lips. And she had felt so full of love at his uncharacteristic spontaneity that she had thrown her arms around him and given him a really terrific hug, at least by pregnancy standards, which was from three feet away.

She shifted on the bed, and her eyelids fluttered open. She caught a glimpse of light from the windows, behind institutional-beige curtains. The brightness told her it was morning, though of which day, she didn't know. Before her eyes closed again, she spotted Jack, a sleeping silhouette slumped in a chair, his broad shoulders slanted down. His head, with his sandy hair rumpled, had fallen to the side; he would have a crook in his neck when he awoke.

She felt an ache of love for him, together with an ache of pain for their loss. His son. Their son. A son could continue to redeem a family name tainted by his grandfather's shady dealings. He had become one of the most respected lawyers in New Orleans, if not Louisiana, and his secret motive was to silence the whispered sniggering behind hands, the malicious talk of Creole mob connections and worse. He'd served on several committees to allocate Katrina relief funds, and his work to help the hurricane victims had gained him some national attention. For him, a baby son represented a new, brighter future.

I'll take one of each, Charley, he said one night, as she rested on his chest after they had made love. He had been tender with her in bed, even more so than usual, moving gingerly over her growing tummy. Neither wanted to do anything to hurt the baby, the two of them as spooked as kittens.

But now there would be no baby, no son, no redemption. Only emptiness.

She blinked, then closed her eyes, feeling tears well. She didn't cry, stopping at the edge of emotion, afraid to fall into the chasm of full-blown grief. The drugs were preventing feelings from reaching her, distancing her even from herself. She must be having some kind of delayed reaction. The night she'd miscarried, she'd been so scared when she heard that she was in danger and Harry, too, that she hadn't had time to react to losing the baby, much less to mourn him.

Her eyelids fluttered again, and the background noise grew louder. She was waking up; there was no avoiding it. She realized that the talking wasn't in the hall, but it was her husband's voice. He was saying, "Don't worry, she's asleep and should be up in an hour or so."

She looked over, her vision clearing, and realized that he hadn't been asleep, but on the cell phone, which was tucked in his neck.

"Okay, good luck," he said into the phone. "I'll keep you posted."

"Jack?" she asked, her voice raspy.

"Hey, sleepyhead." He closed the phone, rose, and came over to the bed with a warm smile. "How you feeling?"

"Fine." She didn't feel like telling the truth, not now.

"That was your dad, checking on you." He sat on the bed and stroked her hair back from her forehead. "Good news. He's fine. He's joined forces with some people he seems to have faith in. I gotta believe he knows what he's doing."

"He does." She felt relief wash over her. A professional, her father knew who to trust and who to run from.

Perez leaned over and gave her a soft kiss. "So all we have to worry about now is you."

Suddenly a burst of laughter came from the open door, and they both looked up in time to see a stout nurse in patterned scrubs bustle into the room, her hand extended palm-up. "Give it here, buddy!" she said to Perez. Her voice was louder than was polite, but she was laughing.

"No way." He laughed, too.

"We had a deal," the nurse shot back, and without missing a beat, she grabbed the cell phone out of his hand. "Your husband works too damn hard," she said. "I told him he can't use his phone in the hospital. Now I'm confiscating it."

Perez rose, mock-frowning. "Who are you supposed to be? Nurse Ratchett?"

"You know, your poor husband hasn't eaten since yesterday lunch," the nurse said. "He won't leave your side."

"Aww." She felt a pang of guilt. The nurse

couldn't know that Jack was guarding her in case the killer came looking for them.

"All the other girls are crushing on him, but I'm impervious to his charms."

"Impossible," Perez said with a smirk.

She was feeling safer now that it was morning and her father was OK. Plus the hospital was waking up, the hallway increasingly noisy. "Jack," she said, "why don't you go get some breakfast? Take a break."

"No, I'm fine." He dismissed her with a wave but the nurse grabbed his arm.

"Go, get out. I have to check some things on your wife, and I'd throw you out, anyway."

Perez said, "You OK, Charley?"

"Yes. Please, go. Eat something."

Perez nodded, then eyed the nurse with amusement. "Gimme my phone, Ratchett."

"When you come back."

"But I need to make calls."

"Go and take a break."

"Sir, yes, sir." Perez mock-saluted as he left.

"So how are you doing?" the nurse asked. She had a pleasantly fleshy face, with animated blue eyes and a freckled nose, and she wore her wiry, reddish hair back in an unfashionably long ponytail.

"Fine, I guess." She wasn't about to open up about her feelings to someone she hardly knew. The nurse tugged over a rolling cart, slid out a digital thermometer, and replaced its plastic tip.

"Open wide."

She obeyed like a baby bird, and the nurse stuck the thermometer into her mouth.

"You slept well, and your color looks good. I need to check your vitals."

The thermometer beeped. The nurse slid it out, read it quickly, then replaced it in the cart.

"You're back to normal," she said.

"Great. Is that what you have to check out on me?"

"No, I just said that to give us some alone time." The nurse took the blood pressure cuff from a rack on the wall and began wrapping it around her patient's upper arm. "I wanted to see how you were feeling. Really feeling, I mean. It's tough, emotionally, I know. I missed once, myself."

Missed. That must be the lingo.

"You will get through this, I promise. Take your time." The nurse squeezed the black rubbery bulb, and the pressure cuff got tighter and tighter.

"Excuse us, ladies!" called a voice from the door. A doctor entered, and two interns followed like a flying wedge of white coats.

"You're early, doc," the nurse said, her smile fading. She let the cuff deflate rapidly.

"Our chief weapon is surprise," the doctor said, and the young interns laughed.

"Please, no more Monty Python." The nurse rolled her eyes, folded up the blood pressure cuff, and stuffed it back in the wire rack. "I can't take any more."

"Ha! And now for something completely different." The doctor approached the bed with a sly smile, and the interns laughed again.

"Get ready to fake-laugh, Mrs. Perez," the nurse said as she patted her arm. "They're men, so they'll buy it." She handed over a cell phone. "Oh, I almost forgot, here's your hubby's phone."

"Thanks," she said, not recognizing it as Jack's. He must have gotten a new one.

"See ya, wouldn't wanna be ya." The nurse hustled from the room.

"I'm Dr. Lehmann, and these are my interns, but you don't have to know their names. Think of them as Palin and Gilliam to my John Cleese."

She fake-laughed, and the nurse was right. He bought it. Dr. Lehmann had a square jaw and long nose, and he smelled of fresh cologne. His expression was warm—until it changed.

"Well, my dear, you've been through hell."

"Yes."

"We did get some reports back, which we need to talk with you about." Dr. Lehmann frowned almost sternly, a pitchfork folding in the middle of his forehead, under steel gray hair like Brillo. "Your blood work shows unusual hormone levels, consistent with certain medications. Have you taken anything we should know about?"

She blinked, confused. "No, not at all."

"Nothing?"

"Nothing at all. I won't even take a baby aspirin."

"Really?"

"Really."

"Well." Dr. Lehmann frowned at her over the steely top of his glasses. "I won't mince words. To be frank, your levels are consistent with someone who has taken RU 486."

She didn't understand.

"Mifeprex. It's best administered under medical supervision. But unfortunately, it's commonly self-administered by women who want to induce miscarriage, much later in their pregnancy. It's commonly known as the abortion pill."

She couldn't see where he was going. "Okay, but what does that have to do with me?"

"Perhaps you wanted to end your pregnancy."

"Me? No. No way." She felt stricken. "Never."

Dr. Lehmann eyed her, plainly doubtful. "Many people who administer the pill themselves in the later trimesters don't realize that it's very dangerous and could lead to extreme loss of blood, which is what happened in your case. You could have bled to death."

"You think I tried to give myself an abortion?"

"Yes, I do. You can tell me the truth or not. Up to you." Dr. Lehmann paused as if for a confession.

"Is that why I miscarried?"

"Yes."

"How can you be sure?"

"Your levels can be explained by only one thing. In fact, they suggest you took two pills. You wouldn't be the first woman to have thought of that, either. Still, it's very, very dangerous."

"No, that's not what happened! I did not take the pill, any pill. I never would. I wanted this baby."

"I'm merely telling you what your blood work reveals."

"Then it's not my blood work. There's been a mistake." She looked at his lined face, then the equally grave faces of the interns. "There must have been a mistake."

"Look, Mrs. Perez, this is your business. I want to emphasize to you that it would be unwise to ever do this again." Dr. Lehmann's expression softened. "No judgment here. I'm concerned only for your safety."

She tried to function. "How does it cause an abortion, this pill?"

"The bottom line is that after the pill is ingested, severe cramping occurs and the fetus is expelled. When medically unsupervised, as in your case, it necessitates a D&C to be complete." Dr. Lehmann checked his watch. "We must be going. Grand rounds this morning. We'll check on you later."

She watched them go in silence. After they had left, her thoughts tumbled over one another, fast and furious. She hadn't taken an abortion pill, much less two. But she'd had cramping that night,

208

so severe she'd doubled over from them. The cramps had started sometime after dinner.

She thought back to that awful night. She and Jack had had their typical Friday night dinner, which he routinely cooked as an end-of-the-week treat for her. He'd made chicken with rosemary and mashed potatoes, her favorite. He even shooed her from the kitchen when she'd tried to help and had served it to her at her seat, doling out extra mashed potatoes, over her protest.

The memory made her heart stop.

No.

She shook her head. It didn't make sense. It couldn't make sense. The blood work had to be wrong. Any other possibility was unthinkable. Impossible. There had to be a mistake.

She tried to puzzle it out, turning the cell phone over and over in her hand. Its smooth metallic finish caught the light from the harsh overhead fluorescents, and she flipped it open on impulse. The tiny, multicolored screen showed the menu and on impulse, she pressed the button for the call logs. On the screen appeared a sharp-focus highlighting of the last call that had been received. It should have shown that it was her father, but the caller's name didn't read DAD or even HARRY.

Instead, it read: MOZART.

Huh?

Why would Jack call her father Mozart? Puzzled, she flipped through the menu to the address book and skimmed the address list. The names were in alphabetical order, and she skimmed them: BACH, BEETHOVEN, BRAHMS, CHOPIN, HANDEL, LISZT, MAHLER, MENDELSSOHN, SCARLATTI, SCHUBERT, SCHUMANN, SHOSTAKOVICH, SIBELIUS, TCHAIKOVSKY, VIVALDI.

What?

They were all composers. But Jack didn't know anything about music; her father was the music expert. What was going on? It looked as if the names were some kind of code, on a cell phone she hadn't even known existed.

What was happening? Who was Mozart? Had Jack heard from Harry? Had he lied about that? Why would he? Was Harry really okay? Suddenly, she didn't understand anything. The miscarriage. The abortion pills. A secret phone with coded addresses. Her heart thundered in her chest. Her mouth went dry. She needed answers.

She pressed the button for MOZART, thumbed back to the call log, and pressed the button for the MOZART profile. It contained no real name, no email and no other information except for the phone number, which had too many digits. What did that mean? Then she realized there was a country code in front of the number. She didn't know which country it was, but she knew it was an international number.

She pressed the buttons for two more profiles,

HANDEL and LISZT. Both profiles were international calls, too, with no other information, like real name, email, or home phones. Why would Jack have a cell phone entirely—and solely—of international numbers? He'd never even traveled abroad; she was the world traveler of the two.

What about the baby?

She pushed the button and recalled MOZART, whoever the hell that was. The phone rang three times.

"Vukasin," answered a man, in a thick accent she couldn't identify.

She pressed End, her heart hammering. Who was Vukasin? What was going on? She couldn't puzzle it out fast enough. Something was horribly wrong, and Jack would be back any minute. She didn't know what to do. Confront him? Then she realized that this Vukasin guy could call back and blow her cover.

There was only one thing to do.

She hurled the cell phone to the hospital floor with all her might. The phone's plastic back sprung open, and the slim orange battery flew out, skidding to the wall in front of the chair.

Just then Perez appeared grinning in the doorway. "Honey, I'm home!"

She arranged her face into a wifely mask and turned sheepishly to the door. "Please don't be mad," she said, willing herself to act natural. "The nurse gave me your phone but I dropped it."

"Damn, Charley." Annoyance flickered over his handsome features. "It was a new one."

"I noticed. Sorry." She eased back into bed, watching her husband with new suspicion. "Did you buy one of those insurance contracts for it?"

"No." He strode to the chair, bent down, and began picking up the pieces of the cell phone. "Looks like all the king's horses and all the king's men . . ."

". . . can't put it back together again?" She finished his sentence with ersatz remorse.

"Nah, but that's OK." He slipped the plastic shards of the phone into his jacket pocket and turned to his wife with a smile she had loved so much it broke her heart.

Did you kill our baby?

Did you try to kill me?

But she wouldn't ask him anything, just yet. She had to calculate her next move. Until she knew more, the best course was to keep her mouth shut and her eyes open.

She wasn't Harry Middleton's daughter for nothing.

14

P. J. PARRISH

Kaminski stood at the window staring down at the inner harbor. A fog had rolled in and the lights of the buildings blinked back at her like eyes in the dark.

Her head was pounding—from bone-deep fatigue and the lingering effects of Faust's Champagne. But also from fear.

She had never really felt fear like this before. Not when her parents disappeared and she was left on her own. Not when she had felt the press of the violin string against her neck when the man tried to kill her in Rome. Not even after she found out Uncle Henryk had been murdered.

But an hour ago, seeing the tattooed man bound in the closet, his bald head pouring blood, the cold, hammering fear began. It built as she heard him whimper as Faust whispered in his ear, as she saw his terrified tears, smelled the stench of his urine.

Shivering, she now moved away from the window, rubbing her hands over her arms. She scanned the suite's living room, its oriental carpets and colonial furnishings. A mahogany bar dominated one corner, a gleaming baby grand piano the other. Off to the left, through open French doors, she could see one of the two bedrooms. Faust's Vuitton duffle sat on the four-poster bed.

After the trip to the apartment, Faust had dropped her back at the hotel, and without another word, locked the door behind him and left. The man he called Nacho had been told to watch her. When he finally dozed off in the chair by the door, gun in hand, Kaminski had thought of running.

But where would she go? Faust had taken her passport, the one with the Joanna Phelps name on it, and her money. She knew no one in this country.

No, that wasn't true. She knew of one person: Harold Middleton, who taught at the American University in Washington, D.C., and whose name was on the package containing the Mozart manuscript Uncle Henryk had sent to Signor Abe days before he was murdered.

Kaminski shut her eyes, Abe Nowakowski's offer of help echoing in her head. She had tried to call him again in Rome, but the operator told her there was a block on her phone. No calls in or out. And so she was Faust's prisoner, and she didn't know why.

Nacho stirred, but went back to his snoring.

Kaminski paced slowly across the living room.

Her eyes found the piano in the corner and she went to it.

She ran a hand over the sleek black surface then slowly lifted the keyboard's lid. The keys glowed in the soft light.

Suddenly, the image of her father was in her head. She could almost see his long fingers moving over the keys of the old piano in their home. Her little hands had tried so hard at her lessons to please him.

He had been so disappointed when she chose the violin, her mother's instrument. Almost as if she had chosen her mother over him. But it had never been like that. She had loved her father so much, missed him so much.

And when he died, Uncle Henryk had been there for her to take his place.

Now the tears came. Kaminski did not stop them.

She sat down at the piano.

She played one chord. Then a quick section from a half-forgotten song. The Yamaha had an overly bright sound and a too-light action. But it didn't matter. Just hearing the notes was soothing.

She played a Satie Gymnopedie then started Eine Kleine Nachtmusik, a piece Uncle Henryk had so loved.

She stopped suddenly.

Mozart.

She wiped a hand over her face. The Mozart manuscript Signor Abe had given her: Was this the reason Faust had brought her here?

She glanced over at Nacho, who watched her with tired eyes.

She went quickly to Faust's bedroom. He had said the manuscript was "safe," locked in a closet.

She threw open its louvered doors. The closet was empty. She turned and spotted his slender black briefcase sitting on the bed near the duffle.

There was nothing in it but an automatic gun, with an empty clip nearby, and a copy of Il Denaro. She stared at the date: four days ago. She picked it up and unfolded the paper.

Several yellowed manuscript papers fluttered to the bed. Where better for a man like Faust to hide a priceless Mozart manuscript than in plain sight, bundled in the financial news?

She carefully gathered the pages. Back at La Musica, when she had first seen the manuscript, she hadn't had time to really look at it. But now everything registered. The black scratchings were unmistakable. The fine strokes of faded ink. The distinctive signature. And finally, in the left corner very small: no. 28.

Her heart began to beat fast. She knew there were only twenty-seven catalogued Mozart piano concertos. Many of the originals that had resurfaced after the war were now housed in the Jagiellonska Library in Krakow.

Where had this one come from?

And was it the reason her uncle was dead?

She took the manuscript back to the piano. She sat down, carefully setting the fragile papers before her. She began to play.

The first movement opened with throbbing D minor chords. She had to go slowly, the technical demands way beyond her skills. Her heart was pounding with excitement as she grasped that she might be the first in centuries to play this.

She was sweating by the time she reached the end of the first movement. She stopped suddenly.

My God. A cadenza.

She stared at the notes. Her father had taught her that Mozart himself often injected cadenzas—improvised virtuoso solos—into his music. But he never wrote them down. Modern performers usually filled the gaps with their own improvisations that tried to mimic the master's intent.

She began to play the cadenza. But her ears began to pick up strange discordant sounds. Odd little dissonances and patterns. She could suddenly hear her father's voice speaking to her from behind as she practiced.

With Mozart, my dear, with music so pure, the slightest error stands out as an unmistakable blemish.

Kaminski stopped, her fingers poised over the keys.

There was something very strange about this cadenza.

The restaurant was almost empty. Two waiters stood at discreet attention just beyond a red curtain. Middleton could see from their faces they wanted to go home.

Yet Faust seemed in no hurry to go anywhere.

"So you never suspected anything about the Chopin?" Faust asked.

Middleton wasn't sure how much to tell him. He still didn't trust the man.

He thought suddenly about his interrupted ride to Baltimore with the two dopers Traci and Marcus. How he had made them listen to a Schoenberg recitatif, and Marcus's crack that it sounded like nothing but wrong notes.

All the easier to hid a message in, he had told Marcus.

How hard could it be then to encrypt a code within the mathematical beauty of Chopin?

"As soon as I saw it, I felt something was wrong with it," Middleton said. "But I just chalked it up to a bad forgery."

"Jedynak didn't say anything?" Faust asked.

Middleton shook his head. "When we were going over all the manuscripts, he seemed very interested in the Chopin in particular. He insisted I take it back to the States for authentication. Even though I told him I was sure it was a fake."

"Maybe he was trying to get it safely out of the country. Maybe he was trying to keep it out of the wrong hands."

"Jedynak knew the VX formula was encrypted in it?"

Faust shrugged.

Middleton sat back in his chair. "So I was supposed to be some fuckin' mule?"

Faust said nothing. Which angered Middleton even more.

"Can I see it?" Faust asked.

When Middleton didn't move, Faust gave him a sad smile. "I told you. I am desperate. I need your help."

Middleton reached down to the briefcase at his feet and pulled out the manuscript. He handed it to Faust across the table.

Faust looked at it for a moment then his dark eyes came back up to Middleton.

"I know chemistry. You know music." He pushed it across the table. "Tell me what you see."

Middleton hesitated then turned the manuscript so he could read it. The paper and ink alone were enough for him to offer Jedynak his initial opinion that it was probably a forgery. A good one, yes, but still a forgery.

But now, he concentrated on the notes themselves. He took his time. The quiet bustle of the waiters clearing the cutlery and linen fell away. He was lost in the music.

He looked up suddenly.

"There's something missing," he said.

"What do you mean?" Faust asked.

Middleton shook his head. "It's probably nothing. This is, after all, just a forgery. But the end of the first movement—a piece of it is missing."

"But you're not sure," Faust asked.

"I wish I had . . ."

"You wish you had another expert eye?"

"Yes," Middleton said.

"I have one for you," Faust said. "Come. Let's go . . . But we go alone. Not with any visitors."

"Who else would go with us?"

Faust smiled and glanced toward the front of the restaurant, where Tesla and Lespasse awaited. "Alone . . . That is one of the immutable terms of the deal."

"I'll follow your lead."

Faust reached forward and tugged on Middleton's tiny wire microphone/ earbud unit. He dropped it on the floor and crushed it. He then paid the bill. "Wait here." He made a phone call from the pay phone near the men's room then returned to the table. No more than five minutes later sirens sounded in the distance, growing closer. The attention of everyone in the restaurant turned immediately to the front windows. Then, in a flurry of lights and horns, police cars and emergency trucks skidded to a stop across the quaint street from the restaurant, in front of a bar. The bomb squad was the centerpiece of the operation.

Middleton had to give Faust credit. Not a single person in the restaurant or outside was focused anywhere but on the police action. They'd discover soon enough it was a false alarm, but the distraction would serve its purpose.

Middleton slipped the Chopin manuscript back

into his briefcase and rose to his feet. Faust gestured to the kitchen.

"Through the back. Hurry. Time is short."

This was where Felicia Kaminski was, M. T. Connolly thought, and it was where Middleton and Faust would continue their rendezvous.

Connolly now knew what Middleton had that so many people had deemed valuable enough to kill for: a seemingly priceless manuscript created for pleasure but now corrupted with the possibility of mass murder.

Even sitting alone, outside this hotel, in the dark privacy of her own thoughts, she was a little ashamed to admit she was ignorant of the strange history of this Chopin score, and of the human value of such a find. More so, until tonight, she had been as unaware as most Americans about the tragedies at St. Sophia.

But she did understand a monster's need for glory, no matter how twisted and unimaginable it might be to a sane person. And it was an interesting side note to the events of the last few days. Her colleagues in law enforcement were looking for Middleton because they believed he killed two cops. But, thanks to Josef, her angel in Poland, she knew better. Middleton had in his hands a formula for mass destruction, and though he had formed an alliance with Kalmbach and Chambers, she believed he needed her help to keep it away from

Vukasin. Kalmbach and Chambers she did not trust. In the core of her being, she believed the only way to stop a chemical attack within the borders of the United States was to keep Harold Middleton alive.

She took a quick look along the street and checked her watch. There was no sense in going inside the hotel until Middleton and Faust arrived—because it was only then that Vukasin would appear. She had left her previous post inside the restaurant only seconds before Middleton and Faust, sure they would come here to confer with Kaminski, who could help them solve their puzzle.

Now the street was asleep and silent, few lights reflecting life, except in the windows of the Harbor Court Hotel. A white BMW sat under a flickering streetlamp, parked where it could easily be seen. About 100 feet to the south, tucked into the shade of an old oak, was a charcoal sedan, its hood glittering with raindrops, its side windows fogged: Connolly's.

Vukasin was hidden in the generous gray shadows of a nearby building, watching her. He would not move until she did.

Nine minutes later, he was rewarded for his patience. An almost undetectable shift of the undercarriage told him she had readjusted to a more comfortable position. He was certain she had been in the sedan's quiet and security for too long.

Though he rather it had been Middleton or Faust

behind the wheel, or even Kaminski, it mattered little who was in the car. It could be an innocent soul waiting for a lover, or a fool sleeping off the last taste of cheap whiskey. A minor distraction, at best. But one that had to be dealt with. He could not afford to be seen.

Vukasin slipped from his invisibility and made his way toward the sedan. He added a stagger to his walk and a slump to his shoulders to simulate the last journey of a drunk's long night.

The sedan jostled again as Vukasin neared it, the occupant coming to life. He could not see inside as he passed, but he heard the faint creak of wet glass moving as the occupant cracked the window a sliver to see who was passing.

He decided to play.

He ambled back to the sedan, arms spread. "Good evening, kind sir, could you spare a few dollars and direct me to the nearest bus line?"

"Go away," Connolly said, her thoughts on Middleton and the manuscript.

Vukasin moved closer. "I am harmless, I assure you," he said.

"Get the fuck out of here. Go."

The window slipped lower, exposing a pale feminine face, her hair brassy and close-cropped. "I'm a cop," she said. "Now get moving."

"So maybe you'd like a drink?" he asked, as he reached into his pocket. "I have a bottle of Russkaya—"

He saw something begin to crystallize in her eyes as he started to withdraw the automatic.

She knows, he thought, with a smile. She knows I'm not American and not a drunk just passing by.

Her eyes widened in complete understanding.

She knew who he was.

And when she saw the metallic glint of the Glock leveled at her head, she knew she was about to die.

He fired, the silenced shot sounding like no more than a small but powerful puff of hot air on the empty street.

15

LEE CHILD

They used the Harbor Court's main street door.
Faust led the way to it and pulled it and let
Middleton walk through first. Good manners, eti-
quette, and a clear semaphore signal to the hotel's
front-of-house staff: I'm a guest and this guy is
with me. A literal embrace, one hand holding the
door and the other shepherding Middleton inside.
A commonplace dynamic, repeated at the hotel's
entrance a thousand times a day. The staff looked
up, understood, glanced away.

Vukasin didn't glance away. From 40 yards his
gaze followed both men to the elevator bank.

The elevator was smooth but slow, tuned for a low-
rise building. Faust got out first, because
Middleton wouldn't know which way to turn.
Faust held his arms at a right angle, like a traffic
cop, blocking right, pointing left. Middleton
walked ahead. Thick carpet, quiet air. The muffled
sound of a piano. A bright tone and a fast, light
action. A Yamaha or a Kawai, Middleton thought.
A grand, but not a European heavyweight. A
Japanese baby, cross-strung. Light in the bass,
tinkly in the treble. A D-minor obbligato was being
played confidently with the left hand, and a hesi-

tant melody was being played with the right, in the style of Mozart. But not Mozart, Middleton thought. Certainly no Mozart he had ever heard before. Sight-read, which might explain the hesitancy. Perhaps a pastiche. Or an academic illustration, to demonstrate the standard musicological theory that Mozart bridged the gap between the classical composers and the romantics. The melody seemed to be saying: See? We start with Bach, and 200 years later we get to Beethoven.

The sound got louder but no clearer as they walked. Faust eased ahead and repeated his traffic-cop routine outside a door, blocking the corridor, corralling Middleton to a stop. Faust took a key card from his pocket. It bottomed in the slot, a red light turned green, and the mechanism clicked.

Faust said, "After you."

Middleton turned the handle before the light clicked red again. Bright piano sound washed out at him. The melody again, started over from the top, played this time with confidence, its architecture now fully diagrammed, its structure understood.

But still not Mozart.

Middleton stepped inside and saw a suite, luxurious but not traditional. A lean, bearded man in a chair by the door, with a gun in his hand. His nickname, it turned out, was Nacho. A Yamaha baby grand, with a girl at the keyboard. Manuscript pages laid out left-to-right in front of her on the piano's lid. The girl was thin. She had dark hair and a pinched Eastern European face full of a thousand sorrows. The manuscript looked to be a handwritten original. Old foxed paper, untidy notations, faded ink.

The girl stopped playing. Middleton's mind filled in what would come next, automatically, to the end of the phrase. Faust stepped in behind Middleton and closed the door. The room went quiet. Faust ignored the man in the chair. He walked straight to the piano and gathered the manuscript pages and butted them together and left them in a tidy pile on a credenza. Then he stepped back and closed the lid on the piano's keyboard, gently, giving the girl time to remove her fingers. He said, "Time for business. We have a Chopin manuscript."

"Forged and faked," Middleton said.

"Indeed," Faust said. "And missing a page, I think. Would you agree?"

Middleton nodded. "The end of the first movement. Possibly not a whole page. Maybe just sixteen bars or less."

"How many notes?"

"That's an impossible question. It's a concerto. A dozen instruments, sixteen bars, there could be hundreds of notes."

"The solo instrument," Faust said. "The theme. Ignore the rest. How many notes?"

Middleton shrugged. "Forty, maybe? A statement, a restatement, a resolution. But it's still an impossible question. It isn't Chopin. It's somebody pretending to be Chopin."

Faust said, "I think that helps us. We have to second-guess a second-guesser. It's about what's plausible."

"We can't compose the end of something that didn't exist in the first place."

Faust opened his jacket and took a folded glassine envelope from the inside pocket. Unfolded it and smoothed it. Behind the milky acetate was a single sheet of paper. It had been torn out of a reporter's note pad. It was speckled with dried brown bloodstains. Small droplets. Not arterial spray. Just the kind of spatter that comes from small knife wounds, or heavy blows to a face. Under the stains the paper had been ruled by hand into music staves. Five lines, four spaces, repeated four times. A treble clef. E-G-B-D-F. Every Good Boy Deserves Favor. A 4/4 time signature. Sixteen measures. A melody, sketched in with deft untidy strokes of a pen.

Faust laid the page in front of the girl, on the piano's lid, where the Mozart had been. He said, "Suppose someone who had seen the missing page was asked to reproduce what had been there."

The girl looked at the spatters of blood and said, "Asked?"

Faust said, "Required, then."

The girl said, "My uncle wrote this."

"You can tell?"

"It's handwritten. Handwriting is handwriting, whether it's words or musical notes."

Middleton said, "Your uncle?"

Faust said, "This is Felicia Kaminski. Temporarily going as Joanna Phelps, but she's Henryk Jedynak's niece. Or, she was." Then he pointed at Middleton and addressed the girl and said, "And this is Colonel Harold Middleton. He saw your uncle in Warsaw. Your uncle was a brave man. He stole a page. He knew what was at stake. But he didn't get away with it."

"Who did this to him?"

"We'll get to that. First we need to know if he put the truth on paper."

Faust took out the rest of the first-movement manuscript and handed it to the girl. She spread it out in sequence. She followed the melody with her finger, humming silently. She raised the piano's lid again and picked out phrases on the keys, haltingly. She jumped to the bloodstained page and continued. Middleton nodded to himself. He heard continuity, logic, sense.

Until the last measure.

The last measure was where the movement should have come home to rest, with a whole note that settled back to the root of the native key, with calm and implacable inevitability. But it didn't. Instead it hung suspended in midair with an absurd discordant trill, sixteenth notes battling it out through the whole of the bar, a dense black mess on the page, a harsh beating pulse in the room.

The girl said, "The last bar can't be right."

Faust said, "Apparently."

The girl played the trill again, faster. Said, "OK, now I see."

"See what?"

"The two notes are discordant. Play them fast enough, and the intermodulation between them implies a third note that isn't actually there. But you can kind of hear it. And it's the right note. It would be very obvious on a violin."

Middleton said, "Chopin didn't write like that."

The girl said, "I know."

Faust asked, "What's the implied note?"

The girl played the trill for half a bar and then stabbed a key in between and a pure tone rang out, sweet and correct and reassuring. She said, "Two notes."

Faust said, "Sounds like one to me."

"The last note of this movement and the first of the next. That's Chopin. Who did this to my uncle?"

Faust didn't answer, because right then the door opened and Vukasin walked in. He had a silenced Glock held down by his thigh and from six feet away Middleton could smell that it had been used, and recently. Faust said, "We're all here." He made the formal introductions, one to the other, Vukasin, Middleton, Nacho, Kaminski. He let his gaze rest on Kaminski and said, "Colonel Middleton killed your uncle. He tortured that page out of him and then cut his throat. In Warsaw, after their lunch."

"Not true," Middleton said.

"True," Vukasin said. "I saw him leave. I went in and found the body. Three bodies. Two bystanders got in the way, apparently."

Faust stepped aside as Nacho took Middleton's arms and pinned him. Vukasin raised the silenced Glock and pointed it at Middleton's face. Then Vukasin lowered the gun again and reversed it in his hand and offered it butt-first to the girl. Said, "Your uncle. Your job, if you want it."

The girl got up off the piano stool and stepped around the end of the keyboard and came forward. Took the gun from Vukasin, who said, "It's ready to go. No safety on a Glock. Just point and shoot, like a cheap camera. There won't be much noise."

Then he stood off to her left. She raised the gun and aimed it where he had aimed it, at the bridge of Middleton's nose. The muzzle wavered a little, in small jerky circles. With the sound suppressor it was a long and heavy weapon.

Middleton said, "They're lying."

The girl nodded.

"I know," she said.

She turned to her left, twisting from the waist, and shot Vukasin in the face. He had been right. There wasn't much noise. Just a bang like a heavy book being slammed on a table, and a wet crunch as the bullet hit home, and the soft tumble of a body falling on thick carpet. Then nothing, just the stink of gunpowder and pooling blood.

The girl twisted back, and lined up on Faust.

"Middleton understands music," she said. "I can see that from here. He wouldn't need to torture that melody out of anyone. It was predictable. Like night follows day."

Faust said, "I didn't know."

"The two discordant notes," the girl said. "Making a phantom third. My uncle always called it a wolf tone. And Vukasin means wolf, in Polish. It was a coded message. He was naming his killer."

"I didn't know," Faust said again. "I swear."

"Talk."

"I hired Vukasin. Someone else must have gotten to him. Hired him out from under me. He was double crossing me."

"Who?"

"I don't know. I swear. And we can't waste time on this. The music holds more code than who killed your uncle."

"He's right, Felicia," Middleton said. "First things first. It's about nerve gas. It could make 9/11 look like a day at the beach."

"And it's coming soon," Faust said.

Kaminski nodded.

"Days away," she said.

She lowered the gun.

"Forty notes," Faust said. "Forty letters between A and G. It's not enough."

"Add in the Mozart cadenza," Kaminski said. "That's bullshit too."

Middleton said, "Mozart didn't write cadenzas."

Kaminski nodded. "Exactly. He didn't write twenty-eight piano concertos, either. The cadenza is part of the message. Same board, same game."

Faust asked, "Which first?"

"Mozart. He was before Chopin."

"Then how many notes?"

"The two things together, a couple hundred in total, maybe."

"Still not enough. And you can't spell stuff out using only A through G. Especially not in German."

"There are sharps and flats. The Mozart is in D-minor."

"You can't sharpen and flatten letters of the alphabet."

"Numbers," Middleton said. "It's not letters of the alphabet. It's numbers."

"One for A, two for B? That's still not enough. This thing is complex."

"Not one for A," Middleton said. "Concert pitch. The A above middle C is 440 cycles per second. Each note has a specific frequency. Sharps and flats, equally. A couple hundred notes would yield eighty-thousand digits. Like a bar code. Eighty-thousand digits would yield all the information you want."

Faust asked, "How do we work it out?"

"With a calculator," Middleton said. "On the treble stave the second space up is the A above middle C. That's 440 cycles. An octave higher is the first overtone, or the second harmonic, 880 cycles. An octave lower is 220 cycles. We can work out the intervals in between. We'll probably get a bunch of decimal places, which is even better. The more digits, the more information."

Faust nodded. Nothing in his face. He retrieved the Mozart manuscript from the credenza and butted it together with the smeared page in the glassine envelope. Clamped the stack under his arm and nodded to Nacho. Then he looked at Kaminski and Middleton and suddenly leapt forward, ripping the silenced Glock from her hand.

He said, "I wasn't entirely honest before. I didn't hire Vukasin. We were both hired by someone else. For the same purpose. Which isn't entirely benevolent, I'm afraid. We have ricin, and everything else we need. But we couldn't stabilize the mixture. Now we can, thanks to your keen insights. For which we thank you. We'll express our thanks practically—with mercy. Exactly ten minutes from now, when I'm safely away, Nacho will shoot you both in the head. Fast and painless, I promise."

The gun in Nacho's hand came up and rested level, steady as a rock. He was back in his chair, solidly between Middleton and the door.

Kaminski gasped and caught Middleton's arm. Faust smiled once, and his blue eyes twinkled, and he let himself out.

Ten minutes. A long time, or a short time, depending on the circumstances. Ten minutes in a line at the post office seems like an eternity. The last 10 minutes of your life seems like a blink of an eye. Nacho didn't move a muscle. He was like a statue, except that the muzzle of his gun moved to track every millimetric move that Middleton or Kaminski made, and except that about once every 90 seconds he glanced at his watch.

He took his final look at the time and raised his gun a little higher. Head height, not gut height. His finger whitened on the trigger.

Then the door opened.

Jack Perez stepped into the room.

Nacho turned toward him. Said, "What—"

Perez raised his gun and shot Nacho in the face. No silencer. The noise was catastrophic. They left by the fire stairs, in a big hurry.

Ten minutes later they were in an Inner Harbor diner and Perez was saying, "So basically you told him everything?"

Kaminski nodded her head very ruefully and said, "Yes."

Middleton shook his head very definitively and said, "No."

"So which is it?" Perez said. "Yes or no?"

"No," Middleton said. "But only inadvertently. I made a couple of mistakes. I guess I wasn't thinking too straight."

"What mistakes?"

"Concert pitch is a fairly recent convention. Like international time zones. The idea that the A above middle C should be tuned to 440 cycles started way after both Mozart and Chopin were around. Back in the day the tunings across Europe varied a lot, and not just from country to country or time to time. Pitch could vary even within the same city. The pitch used for an English cathedral organ in the 1600s could be as much as five semitones lower than the harpsichord in the bishop's house next door. The variations could be huge. There's a pitch pipe from 1720 that plays the A above middle C at 380 cycles, and Bach's organs in Germany played A at 480 cycles. The A on the pitch pipe would have been an F on the organs. We've got a couple of Handel's tuning forks, too. One plays A at 422 cycles and the other at 409."

Perez said, "So?"

"So Faust's calculations will most likely come out meaningless."

"Unless?"

"Unless he figures out a valid base number for A."

"Which would be what?"

"428 would be my guess. Plausible for the

period, and the clue is right there in the Mozart. The 28th piano concerto, which he never got to. The message was hidden in the cadenza. If the 28 wasn't supposed to mean something in itself, they could have written a bogus cadenza into any of the first twenty-seven real concertos."

"Faust will figure that out. When all else fails. He's got the Mozart manuscript."

"Even so," Middleton said. He turned to Kaminski. "Your uncle would have been ashamed of me. I didn't account for the tempering. He would have. He was a great piano tuner."

Perez asked, "What the hell is tempering?"

Middleton said, "Music isn't math. If you start with A at 440 cycles and move upward at intervals that the math tells you are correct, you'll be out of tune within an octave. You have to nudge and fudge along the way. By ear. You have to do what your ear tells you is right, even if the numbers say you're wrong. Bach understood. That's what The Well-Tempered Klavier is all about. He had his own scheme. His original title page had a hand-written drawing on it. It was assumed for centuries that it was just decoration, a doodle really, but now people think it was a diagram about how to temper a keyboard so it sounds perfect."

Perez took out a pen and did a rapid calculation on a napkin. "So what are you saying? If A is 440, B isn't 495?"

"Not exactly, no."

"So what is it?"

"493, maybe."

"Who would know? A piano tuner?"

"A piano tuner would feel it. He wouldn't know it."

"So how did these Nazi chemists encode it?"

"With a well-tuned piano, and a microphone, and an oscilloscope."

"Is that the only way?"

"Not now. Now it's much easier. You could head down to Radio Shack and buy a digital keyboard and a MIDI interface. You could tune the keyboard down to A equals 428, and play scales, and read the numbers right off the LED window."

Perez nodded.

And sat back.

And smiled.

16

JEFFERY DEAVER

N o leads."
Emmett Kalmbach and Dick Chambers were supervising the search of the suite at the Harbor Court, which had been rented by Faust under a fake name. Naturally, Middleton reflected sourly, cell phone at his ear; the man was a master of covering his tracks.

"Nothing?" he asked, shaking his head to Felicia Kaminski and Jack Perez, who sat across from him in the diner.

"Nope. We've gone over the entire place," Kalmbach said. "And searched Vukasin's body. And some bastard with a weird tattoo. Name is Stefan Andrzej. Oh, and that Mexican your son-in-law took out. But not a goddamn clue where Faust might've gone."

"The binoculars Felicia told us about?" Kaminski had explained about Nacho's game of I-spy out the window, and the bits of conversation that had to do with deliveries and technical information. "They were focused on a warehouse across the street but it was empty."

"So he's taken the chemicals someplace else."

"And we don't have a fucking clue where," the

239

FBI agent muttered. "We'll keep looking. I'll get back to you, Harry."

The line went dead.

"No luck," Middleton muttered. He sipped coffee and finished a candy bar. He told himself it was for the energy; in fact, he mostly needed the comfort of the chocolate. "At least I gave Faust the wrong information about the code in the music. He can only get so far with the gas."

"But with trial and error," Kaminski asked, "he could he come up with the right formula?"

"Yeah, he could. And a lot of people'll die—and the deaths'd be real unpleasant."

They sat silently for a moment then he glanced at Perez. "You looked pretty comfortable with that Beretta." As he had with the Colt when he took down Eleana Soberski.

His son-in-law laughed. "I stayed clear of the family business in Loseiana. "But that doesn't mean I wasn't aware of the family business." A coy smile. "But you know that, right?"

Middleton shrugged. "I ran a check on you, sure. You were marrying my daughter . . . If there'd been a spec of dirt in your closet, Charley wouldn't have a hyphenated name right now."

"I respect looking out for kin, Harry. I'll be the same way with my . . ." His voice faded and he looked down, thinking, of course, of the child they'd almost had. Middleton touched his arm, squeezed.

Kaminski asked, "My uncle knew you as a musicologist, uno professore. But you are much more than that, aren't you?"

"Yes. Well, I was. I worked for the army and the government. Then I had a group that tracked down war criminals."

"Like the man who killed my uncle?"

"Yes."

"You said 'had.' What happened?"

"The group broke up."

"Why?" Perez asked.

Middleton decided to share the story with them. "There was an incident in Africa. The four of us tracked down a warlord in Darfur. He'd been stealing AIDS drugs from the locals and selling children as soldiers. We did an extraordinary rendition—lured him to international waters and were going to fly him back to The Hague for trial. Then our main witnesses against him all died quote accidentally in a fire. They were in a safe house. The doors were locked and it burned. Most of them had their families with them. Twenty children died. Without the witnesses there was no trial. We had to let him go. I was going to head back to Darfur and make a case against him for the fire but Val—Valentin Brocco—lost it. He heard the man smirking about how he'd beaten us. Val pulled him out back and shot him in the head.

"I couldn't keep going after that. I disbanded the group. You've got to play by the rules. If you don't, their side wins. We're no better than they are."

"It looks like it bothered you very much," Kaminski said.

"They were my friends. It was hard."

And one of them was much more than just a friend. But this was part of the story Middleton didn't share.

His phone beeped. He glanced at the screen and read the lengthy SMS message. "Speak of the devil . . . It's Lespasse and Nora," he explained. "This is interesting . . . They talked to one of our old contacts. He found out that machinery that could be used to make a bio-weapon delivery system was shipped to a factory in downtown Baltimore yesterday." He looked up. "I've got an address. I think I'll go check it out." He said to Perez, "You take Felicia someplace safe and—"

The man shook his head. "I'm going with you."

"It's not your fight, Jack."

"These are terrorists. It's everybody's fight. I'm with you."

"You sure about that?"

"You're not going anywhere without me."

Middleton gave him an affectionate nod. He then subtly pulled his service Glock from his waistband and, holding the gun under the table, checked the ammunition. "I'm short a few rounds. Let me see your Beretta."

Perez slipped him the weapon, out of sight.

Middleton looked over the clip. "You've got twelve and one in the hole. I'm going to borrow three or four."

"Ah, you don't have to pay me back," his son-in-law said, grim-faced. Then smiled. "Give 'em to Faust instead."

Middleton laughed.

They left the diner and walked Kaminski to a hotel up the street. Middleton gave her some money and told her to check in and stay out of sight until they called.

"I want to go," she protested.

"No, Felicia."

"My uncle's dead because of this man."

He smiled at her. "This isn't your line of work. Leave it to the experts."

Reluctantly she nodded and turned toward the hotel lobby.

Middleton climbed into the driver's seat of Perez's car and together the men sped over streets that grew progressively rougher as cobblestones showed through the worn asphalt.

He said, "The delivery was to Four Thirty Eight West Ellicott Street. It's about a mile from here." Middleton then glanced to his right. Perez was shaking his head, smiling.

The father-in-law squinted in curiosity. "What?"

"Funny. You and your friends."

"Who? Lespasse and Nora?"

"Yeah."

243

"What about them?"

The voice was now sharp with sarcasm. "Supposed to be so fuckin' good at your job. And here you are, chasing down a bum lead."

"What're you talking about?"

The Beretta appeared fast. Middleton flinched as he felt the muzzle against his neck. His son-in-law took the Glock, tossed it in the back, along with Middleton's cell phone. Then he undid his father-in-law's seat-belt, but kept his own hooked.

"What's going on?" Middleton gasped.

"The gas delivery system was shipped to Virginia, not Baltimore. We drove it up. Whatever's on Ellicott Street, it doesn't have anything to do with us."

"Us?" Middleton whispered. "You're with them, Jack?"

"'Fraid so, Dad. Turn right here. Head to the waterfront."

"But—"

The black automatic prodding Middleton's ear. "Now."

He did as he was told, following directions to a deserted pier, lined with old warehouses. Perez ordered him to stop. The pistol never wavering, he directed Middleton out of the car and pushed him through an old doorway.

Faust glanced up as if they were guests right on time for a party. In overalls, wearing thick gloves, he was standing at a cluttered worktable littered with tools, tubing and electronic or computer parts. A pallet of gas tanks was nearby. There were 50 or so of them. "Danger—Biohazard" was printed on them in six languages.

Faust gave a fast appraisal of Middleton. "Search him."

"I already—"

"Search him."

Perez patted him down. "Clean."

Middleton shook his head. "I don't get it . . . Jack shot Nacho."

Faust grimaced. "We had to sacrifice the greasy little prick—so you'd believe Mr. Perez here and give us the real musical code. I doubted you'd be honest with me back there."

"He wasn't," Perez confirmed. "He claimed he wasn't thinking clearly. But I'm sure he was lying. He told me how it works." He explained what Middleton had said about adjusting the pitch of A and using a simple electronic tuning device to decode the formula.

Faust was nodding. "Hadn't considered that. Of course."

Middleton said, "So Jack coming to our rescue in the Harbor Court was all part of the plan."

"Pretty much."

"What the hell is going on?"

"I'm just a businessman, Colonel. The world of terrorism is different now. Too many watch lists, too much surveillance, too many computers. You have to outsource. I've been hired by people who are patriots, idealists, protecting their culture."

"Is that how you describe ethnic cleansing?"

Faust frowned. "Protecting them from impurity is how they describe it. You meddled in their country. You'll pay for that. A hundred thousand people will pay."

"And you, Jack?" Middleton snapped.

The young man gave a grim laugh. "I have my own ideals. But they've got commas and a decimal point. I'm making ten million to keep an eye on you and help them out. Yeah, I went to law school and gave up the family business . . . And it was the worst mistake of my life. Going legit? Bullshit." He gazed at his father-in-law contemptuously. "Look at you, Mr. Harry Middleton . . . The star of military intel, the musical genius . . . Faust led you all over the world like he had you on a leash."

"Jack, we don't have time," Faust said. "I'll try the adjustment to the formula. If it works and we don't need him anymore, you can take care of him."

Middleton said, "Jack, you're willing to kill so many people?"

"I'll donate some of the ten million to a relief fund . . ." A grin. "Or not."

Then he stopped talking. Cocked his head.

Faust was looking up too.

"Helicopter," the younger man muttered.

But Faust spat out, "No, it's two. Wait, three."

Faust ran to the window. "It's a trap. Police. Soldiers." He glared at Jack. "You led them here!"

"No, I did what we agreed."

Middleton could hear diesels of Jeeps and personnel carriers in the distance, closing in fast. Spotlights shone from on high.

Faust slapped his hand on a button on the wall. The warehouse was plunged into darkness. Middleton lunged for Faust but saw the man's vague form run to a corner of the warehouse, open a trap door and vanish. A few seconds later, a powerboat engine started up.

Hell! Middleton thought. He swept the light switch on. He ran to the trap door. Tried it, but Faust had locked it from below.

Sweating, frantic, Perez pointed his gun at Middleton. "Harry, don't move. You're my ticket out of here."

Middleton ignored him and started for the front door of the warehouse.

"Harry!" Perez aimed at Middleton's head. "I'm not telling you again!"

Their eyes met. Perez pulled the trigger.

Click.

Middleton pulled a handful of bullets from his pocket. He displayed them. When pretending to take just three or four bullets from the clip in the diner, he'd taken them all—and the one in the chamber too.

His eyes bored into the younger man's. "That text message I got earlier? It wasn't from Nora and Lespasse. It was from Charley. 'Green Lantern.' It's our code for an emergency. And she text-messaged me who I was in danger from. You, Jack. I knew you'd lead me to Faust. So I text-messaged Lespasse and Nora and told them to follow me from the diner."

Middleton leapt forward and slammed his fist into Perez's jaw, then easily twisted the automatic away. He dropped a round into the chamber, locked the slide, aimed at his son-in-law.

"Harry, you don't understand. I was just faking. Playing along to find out who was involved. I'm a patriot."

"No. You're a traitor who was willing to murder a hundred thousand citizens . . ." His eyelids lowered. "A hundred thousand and one."

"One?"

"My grandchild. Charley told me what you did. How could you do something like that? How?"

Perez's shoulders slumped. He looked down and gave up all pretense of lying. "A baby didn't fit my new lifestyle."

"And Charley didn't either, did she? So after losing the baby, my daughter was, what? Going to kill herself in despair?"

He didn't answer. He didn't need to. Middleton grabbed him by the collar, forced the trembling man on his knees, touched his forehead with the muzzle. He felt the pressure closing on his index finger.

This man killed your grandchild, was going to kill your daughter. We're in the middle of a take-down, he attacked you . . .

Nobody'll care if you take him out.

Now, do it! Before anybody comes in.

Perez squinted, sealing his miserable eyes. "Please, Harry. Please."

Green shirt, green shirt, green shirt . . .

Middleton lowered the gun. He shoved Perez to his belly on the floor.

The door burst open. A dozen soldiers and men in FBI jackets filed into the room. The agents cuffed Perez as a bio-weapon containment unit, looking like astronauts in their protective gear, headed straight to the gas tanks and equipment on the worktable, sweeping them with sensors. After a few minutes one of them announced, "Nothing's been mixed yet. There's no danger."

A grizzled man in a uniform with major's stripes strode into the room. Major Stanley Jenkins's face was grim.

Oh, no . . . Middleton deduced what the man had just learned.

"Colonel, sorry. He got away."

Middleton sighed.

Well, at least they'd secured the nerve gas. The city was safe.

And Faust would be the subject of one of the

most massive manhunts in U.S. history. They'd find him. Middleton would make sure of that.

A half hour later, Jack Perez was in detention and Middleton was outside with Tesla, Lespasse and Jenkins—his former colleague from the Army. A car pulled up. Unmarked. Did the feds think people didn't recognize wheels like that? It might as well have had We Serve and Protect in bold type on the side.

Two men climbed out. One was Dick Chambers, the Homeland Security man, and the other FBI Assistant Director Kalmbach.

"Emmett."

"Colonel, I—"

Chambers interrupted. "I don't know what to say, Harry. Your country owes you a huge debt. You saved thousands of lives."

Middleton hoped Kalmbach was used to being snubbed. After stumbling and letting Vukasin and his boys into the country, Chambers was going to milk the win for everything he could.

He added, "We have to debrief you now. We'd like—"

"No," Middleton said firmly. "Now I have to go see my daughter."

"But, Colonel, I have to talk to the director and the White House."

But all that Chambers was talking to at the moment was Harry Middleton's back.

• • •

She would be fine.

Physically, at least. The mental battering from losing her child and the betrayal of her husband was taking its toll, though, and Middleton had whisked her away to the lake house.

They spent a lot of time in front of the TV, watching the news. As he'd predicted, Dick Chambers and other officials from Homeland Security took most of the credit for stopping the nerve-gas attack and finding the terrorists who'd slipped into the country—"owing to extremely well-done forged papers," he pointedly added. The FBI got credited in a footnote.

Harry Middleton was mentioned not at all.

Which was, of course, how this game worked.

The post-mortem of the case suggested that Faust was in charge of the plot to seek revenge against America for the peace-keeping operation. Rugova worked for him but got tired of prison and was going to bribe his way out with loot stolen to support the terrorists.

That's why he was eliminated by Vukasin. Stefan Andrzej, the tattooed man, who'd killed Val Brocco, was probably a traitor, and murdered for that reason—and for his incompetence.

The hunt for Faust was continuing at a fervid pace and several leads were beginning to pan out. He still had some unaccounted-for muscle in the country, and records from the prepaid mobile that

Perez had called frequently, presumably Faust's, showed that he made repeated calls to pay phones in a particular area of D.C., where his cohorts apparently lived. Stakeouts and electronic surveillance were immediately put in place.

But Middleton was, at least for the moment, not part of the hunt. He was more interested in his daughter's recovery.

And in reconnecting with Nora Tesla and Jean-Marc Lespasse.

He'd invited them to the lake house for a few days. He wasn't sure that they'd show up, but they had. His daughter seemed to have forgiven Tesla for what she'd thought was the breakup of her mother and father—though she also had clearly come to understand that the divorce was inevitable long before Nora Tesla entered the picture.

But the other issues loomed and at first the conversations among them had been superficial. The subject of the past finally arose, as it often does, and they broached the subject of the Darfur warlord killed by Brocco and the breaking up of the Volunteers because of the incident.

There was no concession by anybody and no apologies but neither was there any defense, and through the miracles of the passage of time—and friendship arising from common purpose—the incident was at last put to rest.

Tesla and Middleton spent some time together, talking much about things of little significance.

They took a long walk and ended up on a promontory overlooking a neighboring lake. A family of deer sprung from the underbrush and galloped away. Startled, she grabbed his hand—and this time didn't remove it.

Not long after the nerve gas was found Middleton got a phone call. Abe Nowakowski—presently under arrest in Rome—had cut a deal with U.S., Polish and Italian prosecutors. In exchange for a reduced sentence he would give up something.

Something extraordinary, as it turned out.

Overnight, a package arrived at Middleton's lake house. He opened it and spent the next two days in his study.

"Holy shit," was his official pronouncement and the first person he told wasn't his daughter, Nora Tesla or JM Lespasse, but Felicia Kaminski, who came to his house in person in reaction to the news.

He displayed what sat on the Steinway in his study.

"And it's not fake?"

"No," Middleton whispered. "This is real. There's no doubt."

In payment for his services to Faust, Nowakowski had been the recipient of what Middleton had now authenticated: a true Chopin manuscript, previously unheard of, apparently part of the trove unearthed by Rugova at St. Sophia church.

It was an untitled sonata for piano and chamber orchestra.

An astonishing find for lovers of music everywhere.

Also, Middleton was amused to learn that Homeland Security officials had leapt on the news and, further brushing up the feds' image after their nerve gas victory, had pushed for a gala world premiere of the piece at the James Madison Recital Hall in Washington, D.C. Middleton called Dick Chambers personally and insisted that Felicia Kaminski be the principal soloist. He agreed without hesitation, saying, "I owe you, Harry." Violin was her main instrument, of course, but as she joked in her lightly accented English, "I know my way around the ivories too."

Middleton laughed. She grew serious then and added, "It's an honor a musician only dreams of." She hugged him. "And I will dedicate my performance to the memory of my uncle."

Nora Tesla, Lespasse and Charlotte would attend, as would much of Washington's cultural and political elite.

Several days before the concert, Charley Middleton found her father in the lake house study, late at night.

"Hey, Dad. What're you up to?"

Dad? Been years since she'd used that word. It sounded odd.

"Just looking over the Chopin. How are you doing, honey?"

"Getting better. Step by step."

She sat down beside him. He kissed her head. She took a sip of his wine. "Tasty." What he used to say to her after sampling her milk at the breakfast table, long, long ago, to get her to drink the beverage.

"It's amazing, isn't it?" she asked, looking over the manuscript.

"To think that Frederic Chopin actually held these sheets. And look there, that scribble. Was he testing the pen? Was he distracted by something? Was it the start of a note to himself?"

Her eyes were gazing out the window at the black sheet that was the still lake. She was crying softly. She whispered, "Does it ever get better."

"Sure, it does. Your life'll get back on track again."

And Harold Middleton thought, Yes, it gets better. Always does. But the sorrow and horror never go away completely.

Green shirt . . . Green shirt . . .

And a sudden thought came to Harry Middleton. He wondered if he'd used Brocco's murder of the Darfur warlord as an excuse—to back away from the fight that he used to believe he was born for. He couldn't save everybody, so he'd stopped trying to save anyone, and retreated into the world of music.

"I'm going to bed. Love you, Dad."

"Night, baby."

When she was gone, Middleton sipped his wine and examined the Chopin again, thinking of a curious irony. Here was a work of art written at a time when music was created largely for the glory of God and yet this piece he was looking at was part of a horrific plot to murder thousands, solely out of vengeful religious fervor.

Sometimes the world was simply mad, Harry Middleton concluded.

17

JEFFERY DEAVER

The men finished the work at midnight.

"I'm exhausted. Are we through?" The language was Serbo-Croatian.

The second man was tired too but he said nothing and looked uneasily at the third, his face dark, his black hair long and swept back.

The man who'd been supervising their handiwork—Faust—told them in a soft voice that, yes, it was all right to leave. He spoke in English.

Once they were gone, he walked through the basement, using a flashlight to inspect what they'd spent the last four hours doing: Running two-inch hose—it was astonishingly heavy, who'd have thought?—through access tunnels from three buildings away. Painstakingly, using silent hand pumps, they'd filled rubber bladders with gasoline, a total of close to 900 gallons of the liquid. Next they placed propane tanks and detonators between the bladders and, most difficult of all, rigged the electronics.

Alone now in the basement of the James Madison recital hall, Faust ran final diagnostic checks on the system. Everything was in order. He allowed himself a fantasy of what would happen later this evening. During the adagio movement at the world premier of the newly discovered Chopin sonata, a unique combination of notes would slip from the microphone above the soloist's piano and be electronically translated into numerical values. These would be recognized by the computer controller as a command to small motors that would open the propane tanks. Then a few minutes later, when the score moved into the vivace movement, another combination of notes would trigger the detonators. The propane would flare, melt the bladders and turn the recital hall instantly into a crematorium.

This elaborate system was necessary because radio, microwave and cell phone jammers were in use in security-minded public venues in D.C. Remote control devices were useless. And timing devices could be picked up in sweeps by supersensitive microphones.

Ironically, Felicia Kaminski herself would be the detonator.

Now Faust hid the bladders, tanks and wires behind boxes. He was satisfied with the plan. Middleton and the government had taken the bait Nowakowski offered them, the manuscript. And it was clear they believed the entire charade, all false information Faust had fed to Jack Perez and Felicia Kaminski—the code in the first manuscript pages, the nerve-gas attack, the binoculars at the Harbor court focused on a warehouse, the mysterious talk about deliveries and chemical formulas, the torture of the tattooed man in the closet . . .

His enemy's defenses were down. He thought of an apt metaphor: They believed the concert was over; they never suspected he'd arranged a spectacular, unexpected crescendo.

Faust now slipped out of the basement, troubled as he pictured Felicia Kaminski dying in the conflagration. He wasn't concerned about the young women herself, of course. He was troubled that, if she used the original score to perform from, the manuscript would be destroyed.

After all, it was easily worth millions of dollars.

The crowds began assembling outside early, the queue stretching well past a construction site next door to the James Madison hall. Many were people without tickets, hoping for scalpers. But this was a world-premiere of Chopin, not pre-season Redskins, so there were no tickets to be had.

Harold Middleton made a brief backstage visit to Kaminski, wished her well and then joined his guests in the lobby: Leonora Tesla, JM Lespasse and his daughter Charley.

He said hello to some of the music professors from Georgetown and George Mason, and a few of the Defense Department and DOJ folks from his past life. Emmett Kalmbach came by and shook his hand. "Where's Dick?" he asked.

Middleton gave a laugh and pointed across the

hall to the head of Homeland Security. "Gave his ticket to his boss."

The FBI man said, "At least I appreciate culture."

"You ever heard Chopin before, Emmett?"

"Sure."

"What'd he write?"

"That thing."

"Thing?"

"You know, the famous one."

Middleton smiled as Kalmbach changed the subject.

The lobby lights dimmed and they entered the auditorium, found their seats.

"Harry, relax" Middleton heard his daughter say. "You look like you're the one performing."

He smiled, noting how she referred to him. The lack of endearment didn't upset him one bit; it was a sign she was recovering.

But as for relaxing: Well, that wasn't going to happen. This was going to be a momentous evening. He was bursting with excitement.

The conductor walked out on stage to wild applause. He then lifted his arm to the right and nineteen-year-old Felicia Kaminski, in a fluid black dress, strode out on stage, looking confident as a pro. She smiled, bowed and stole a glance at Harold Middleton. He believed she winked. She sat down at the keyboard.

The conductor took his place at the stand. He lifted his baton.

• • •

"Dick, something interesting here."

Chambers was in his office at the Department of Homeland Security, working late. He was thinking about the concert and wondering if his boss was appreciative he'd been given the ticket. He looked up.

"Might want to talk to this guy," his straight-arrow aide said.

The caller was a restaurant worker near the James Madison recital hall. As he was leaving work early that morning, he explained, he'd seen a man leave through the hall's side door. He'd gotten into a car near the site. Thinking it seemed suspicious—the hall had been closed all day—he took a picture of the car and the license plate with his cell phone. He meant to call the police earlier but had forgotten about it. He'd just now called D.C. police and was referred to Homeland Security, since the concert would be attended by some high-ranking government officials.

"Nowadays," the restaurant worker said, "you never know—terrorists and everything."

Chambers said, "We better follow up on this. Where are you?"

He'd just gotten off work, the man explained. He gave the address of the restaurant. It was now closed so Chambers told him to wait in a park near the place. He'd have agents there soon.

"And thank you, sir. It's citizens like you that make this country what it is."

On stage at the recital hall, Felicia Kaminski was playing as she'd never played in her life. She was motivated not by the fact that this was her first appearance as a soloist at a world premiere, but because of the music itself. It was intoxicating.

Musicians grow familiar with the pieces in their repertoire, the same way husbands and wives grow comfortably close over the years. But there's something about meeting, then performing, a new work that's like the beginning of a love affair.

Passionate, exhilarating, utterly captivating. The rest of the world ceases to exist.

She was now lost in the music completely, unaware of the thousand people in the audience, the lights, the distinguished guests, the other members of the chamber orchestra around her.

Only one thing intruded slightly.

The faint smell of smoke.

But then she came to a tricky passage in the Chopin and, concentrating hard, she lost any awareness of the scent.

A dark sedan pulled up fast, near a small park in northwest D.C., where a middle-aged man in food-stained overalls sat on a park bench, looking around like a nervous bird.

He flinched when the car stopped and only after spotting the plate Official Government Use and the letters on the side, DHS, did he rise. He walked to the man who got out of the car.

"I'm Joe. From the diner," he said. "I called."

"I'm Dick Chambers." They shook hands.

"Please, sir," the worker said. He held up his cell phone. "I have the picture of the license plate. It's hard to read but I'm sure you have computers that can make it, you know, clearer."

"Yes, our technical department can work miracles."

A man climbed from the car. He called, "Dick, just heard a CNN report on the radio! A fire in the recital hall. It looks big. Real big!"

Dick Chambers smiled, then turned to the man who had just shouted to him from the car.

It was Faust. His two thugs stepped out of back of the car and joined him.

"There, he's the man I saw," cried the agitated restaurant worker. "You have arrested him!"

But then he shook his head, seeing that Faust's hands weren't cuffed. "No, no, no." He dropped the cell phone, staring at Chambers. "You're part of it! I am dead!"

Yeah, you pretty much are, the Homeland Security man thought.

Chambers asked Faust, "What's going on at the hall?"

"They are just preliminary reports. No one can

see anything. The streets are filled with smoke. Fire trucks everywhere."

"The recital hall! You've blown it up?"

He crushed the restaurant worker's cell phone under his heel. "I'm afraid you were at the wrong place at the wrong time." He then glanced at Faust, who pulled out a silenced pistol and began to aim it at the worker.

"Please, sir. No!"

Which is when the spotlights slammed on, fixing Chambers, Faust and the others in searing glare.

The restaurant worker dropped to the grass and scuttled away as a loudspeaker blared, "This is Emmett Kalmbach, Chambers. We've got snipers and they're green lighted to shoot. On the ground. All of you."

The DHS man blinked in shock but he hesitated only a moment. He'd been in this business a long time. He was four pounds of trigger pressure away from dead, and he knew it. He grimaced, dropped to his belly and stretched out his legs and arms. The two thugs did the same.

Faust, though, hesitated, the gun bobbing slowly in his hand.

"You, on the ground now!"

But undoubtedly Faust knew what awaited him—the interrogation, the conviction and either life in jail or a lethal needle—and chose desperate over wise. He fired toward the spotlights, then turned and began sprinting.

The lanky man who'd made a job of running from the consequences of his actions got six feet before the snipers ended his career forever.

Harry Middleton walked forward into the lights set up by the FBI Washington field office crime scene team.

He glanced at Faust's body then shook the hand of the man who'd been their undercover decoy—the one who'd pretended to have seen Faust sneak from the recital hall.

"Jozef. You're okay?"

"Ah, yes," Padlo said. "A scrape on my palm getting under cover. No worse than that."

The Polish inspector was stripping off the restaurant worker's uniform he'd donned for the takedown. He'd flown in that morning. It was true that getting credentials for a foreign law officer to come into America was difficult, but red tape did not exist for men like Harold Middleton and his anonymous supervisors.

Padlo had learned that Faust was instrumental in the death of his lover M. T. Connolly and called Harry Middleton, insisting that he come help to find Faust and his co-conspirators. There'd be no extradition of any perpetrators to Poland, Middleton had said, but Padlo was willing to give the Americans evidence in the Jedynak murders, which could prove helpful in any prosecutions here.

Middleton joined Kalmbach and, flanked by two FBI agents, cuffed Dick Chambers, who was staring at the colonel.

"But . . . The fire. You were . . ." His voice faded.

"Supposed to die? Along with a thousand other innocent people? Well, a team disarmed the bomb this afternoon, pumped the gas out. But we needed to buy some time while we set up this sting. If there was no fire at all, I was afraid you might panic and stonewall. So we lit a controlled fire in the construction site next door to the hall. No damage, but a lot of smoke. Enough to get us some ambiguous breaking news reports.

"Oh, if you're interested, the concert went on as planned. The Chopin piece, by the way, was pretty good . . . I'd rate it A minus. I'm sure your boss enjoyed it. Interesting you gave your ticket to him, knowing that he'd die in the fire. Should have seen his face when I told him it was you who was responsible."

Chambers knew he should just shut up. But he couldn't help himself. He said, "How did you know?"

"Well, this story that Faust was the mastermind? Bullshit. I couldn't believe that. He was too arrogant and impulsive. I had a feeling somebody else was behind it. But who? I had some colleagues run a computer correlation on travel to Poland and Italy in the past few months tied to any connections in that part of D.C. where Faust called pay phones. Some diplomats showed up, some businessmen. And you—who worked for the agency that quote accidentally let Vukasin into the country. I found out you also called Nowakowski in prison the day before he offered to give up the Chopin manuscript.

"You were the number-one suspect. But we needed to make sure. And we had to flush Faust. So we set you up with a phony witness as a decoy. Jozef Padlo, who you'd never met."

"This is ridiculous. You don't know what you're talking about."

"Yeah, I do. Dick. As soon as I got the call from Poland about the first Chopin manuscript, I became suspicious and made some calls. Intelligence from Northern Europeans suggested possible terrorist activity originating in Poland and Rome. Music might have something to do with it. So I went along, to see what was up. The trail led to a possible nerve-gas attack in Baltimore. We got the chemicals and it looked like the end of the story, except for tracking down Faust.

"But I got to thinking about things the other night. An attack out of revenge for our meddling in the Balkans? No, the ethnic cleansing there was about politics and land, not religious fundamentalism. That didn't fit the profile. Maybe Vukasin bought into the ideology but the main players, Faust and Rugova? No, they were all about money.

"And codes of nerve gas in a manuscript? Just

the sort of thing the intelligence gurus would love and keep us from looking at the big picture. But in these days of scramblers and cryptography, there were better ways to get formulae from one country to another. No, something else was going on. But what? I decided I needed to analyze the situation differently. I looked at it the same way I look at music manuscripts to decide if they're authentic: as a whole. Did this seem to be an authentic terrorist plot? No. The next logical question was what did the fake nerve-gas plot accomplish?

"Only one thing: It brought me and the rest of the Volunteers out of retirement. That was your point, of course. To eliminate us. The Volunteers."

It was Kalmbach who asked, "But why, Harry?"

"Close to a billion dollars in stolen art and sculpture and manuscripts—stolen by the Nazis from throughout Europe and stashed in a dozen churches and schools in Kosovo, Serbia and Albania. Just like at St. Sophia. We knew that Chambers did a brief tour in the Balkans but got out fast. He must've met Rugova and learned about the loot. Then he bankrolled the operation and hired Faust to oversee it.

"A few years passed and they wanted to cash in by selling the pieces to private collectors. But Rugova preempted them—and he got careless. He didn't cover his tracks and word got around about the treasures. It was only a matter of time until the Volunteers started to put the pieces together. So

Chambers and Faust had to eliminate Rugova—and us too. But to keep suspicion off them they had to make it seem like part of a real terrorist attack. They brought Vukasin and his thugs over here.

"Well, after I realized his motive, I just looked for what would be the perfect way to kill all of us. And it was obvious: an attack at the recital hall."

Now Middleton turned to Chambers. "I wasn't surprised to find out that you were the one at Homeland Security who suggested the concert, Dick."

"This is all bullshit. And you haven't heard the last of it."

"Wrong on number one. Right on two: I'll be a witness in your trial, so I'll be hearing a lot more of it. And so will you."

Kalmbach and two other agents escorted Chambers and Faust's two thugs away for booking.

Middleton and Inspector Jozef Padlo found themselves standing alone on the chilly street corner. A light drizzle had started falling.

"Jozef, thank you for doing this."

"I would not have done otherwise. So . . . It is finished."

"Not quite. There are a few questions to answer. There's one intriguing aspect I'm curious about: Eleana Soberski. She had a connection to Vukasin. But I think there was more to her. I think she had her own agenda."

He recalled what she said just before she was shot: "We are aware of your relationship with Faust."

"Ah," Padlo said, "so there's someone else interested in the loot. Or perhaps who has some of his own and would like to expand his market share."

"I think so."

"One of Rugova's men?"

Middleton shrugged. "Doubt it. They were punks. I'm thinking higher up. Someone highly placed, like Dick Chambers, but in Rome or Warsaw or Moscow."

"And you are going to find out who?"

"The case is my blood. You know the expression?"

"I do now."

"I'll keep at it until I'm satisfied."

"And are you going to do this alone," asked the Polish cop, with a clever gleam in his eye, "or with the help of some friends?"

Middleton couldn't help but smile. "Yes, we've talked about reuniting, the Volunteers."

Padlo fished in his pocket for a pack of Sobieski cigarettes. He pulled one out. Then frowned. "Oh, in America, is okay?"

Middleton laughed. "Outside in a park? That's still legal."

Padlo lit up, sheltering the match from the mist. Inhaled deeply. "Where do you think the stolen art is, Harry?"

"Faust and Chambers probably have a half-dozen safe houses throughout the world. We'll find them."

"And what do you think you will find there?"

"If the Chopin is any clue, it'll be breathtaking. I can't even imagine."

Middleton glanced at his watch. It was after midnight. Still, this was northwest D.C., a yuppie oasis in the city that often sleeps. "Will you join me for a drink? I know a bar that's got some good Polish vodka."

The inspector smiled, sadly. "I think not. I'm tired. My job is done here. I leave tomorrow. And I must get up early to say farewell to someone. Maybe you know where this is?"

He showed Middleton a piece of paper with the address of a cemetery in Alexandria, Virginia.

"Sure, I can give you directions. But tell you what . . . How about if we go together? I'll drive."

"You would not mind?"

"Jozef, my friend, it would be an honor."

Center Point Publishing
600 Brooks Road ● PO Box 1
Thorndike ME 04986-0001 USA

(207) 568-3717

US & Canada:
1 800 929-9108
www.centerpointlargeprint.com